Hidden Desires

Jessica Gatenby

iUniverse, Inc.
New York   Bloomington

Hidden Desires

iUniverse books may be ordered through booksellers or by contacting:

iUniverse
1663 Liberty Drive
Bloomington, IN 47403
www.iuniverse.com
1-800-Authors (1-800-288-4677)

Because of the dynamic nature of the Internet, any Web addresses or links contained in this book may have changed since publication and may no longer be valid. The views expressed in this work are solely those of the author and do not necessarily reflect the views of the publisher, and the publisher hereby disclaims any responsibility for them.

ISBN: 978-1-4502-4332-2 (sc)
ISBN: 978-1-4502-4331-5 (ebook)

Printed in the United States of America

iUniverse rev. date: 1/14/2011

Prologue

She walked down the dark and dirty hallway of what was called a motel here in the slums. *Twenty-two*, she repeated to herself. She was looking for room twenty-two. She soon came upon the decrepit door, and she drew herself up, looked both ways down the hall, and saw no one in sight. She slid her coat off her shoulders and let it pool around her feet, revealing her lean body. She took a deep breath to calm her nerves and knocked on the door. As it opened, she raked her eyes up the occupant's body. He was lean and strong, with washboard abs; he was chiseled and defined; his face was broad and handsome; he had ice blue eyes that were softened by his honey-colored hair. He was one hell of a man, she thought—a very nice man.

"A little far from the ranch, aren't we, cowgirl?" he asked, causing her to tear her gaze away from his eyes.

She grabbed a firm hold of the lasso at her left hip and quickly fell back into step. "Well, I hear there's a wild bronco that needs a tamin'. A long, good ridin' ought to fix him right up."

"Well, you are right. I'm a little hard up, if you know what I mean." He said, "And a wild ride sure would make things right."

He held a dark gleam in his eyes and stepped back for her to enter the room. She picked up her coat and tossed it on the chair in the corner as she entered.

"Why don't you sit down there, cowboy, I need a good warmin' up before I can ride that bronco right." She motioned toward the bed and tilted her cowboy hat forward.

She wandered over to the radio and found a station that was just right, and she wandered back in front of him and started to sway to the music. She wriggled her hips, slid up and down, and rolled her hips as she swung her lasso. She glided across the floor to him and swayed her hips just inches from his body. He grabbed the lasso, threw it to the ground, and tried to pull her close.

"Not just yet there, pilgrim." She pulled out of his reach. "I need to make sure every part of my body feels good."

She ran her hands up her thighs and caressed her stomach. She could feel the heat firing from his eyes toward her as he watched her dance, and she loved knowing that she could turn him on like that. She ran her hands up and caressed her breasts. With one hand on her hat, she let the other play with her hardened nipples. She moaned with pleasure and soon became wrapped in his arms. He kissed the space between her breasts, and she ran her fingers through his hair, letting her hat fall to the ground. She moaned as his mouth moved all over her chest, and she drew her hands down to his chest. She broke his touch and pushed him back onto the bed, preparing to take control; but he grabbed her belt buckle and pulled her forward. He went to undo her belt, but she stopped him.

"No need, cowboy. Crotch-less chaps," she cooed, loving the surprised grin on his face.

She lowered her hands and undid his belt, and he stood and helped her remove his pants and boxers. *Sweet Lord! Is he ever a lovely man.* He fell back onto the bed, and she bent to remove her boots.

"Leave the boots on!"

His command threw her for a moment, it was so harsh in tone, but once she looked back to his large and erect penis, all was forgotten. She climbed onto the bed and straddled him. She pulled herself up, grabbed a handful of his cock, and let it play at her opening. They moaned in unison, and she continued to play.

"Enough playing, it's time for my ride!" He thrust up into her with such force that she gasped.

He moaned with pleasure, and she felt him further swell inside of her. She slid up his shaft and gave a cry of bliss as he nearly exited her. She pushed and pulled as he moaned away, thrusting up into her. With one great thrust, he eliminated her need to play, and she started to drive up and down. She began riding him faster and faster; she could feel herself tightening around him. Their screams filled the room as the bed rattled and squeaked in the background. She was riding him so hard she thought she was going to come apart at the seams, but then suddenly from behind, she felt hands reach around and start to fondle her breasts. She cried out in pleasure and started to pump even harder. The hands massaged her breasts and played with her nipples. She arched her back into the man behind her, allowing her cowboy to hit her G-spot over and over.

"Oh, god, yes!" she cried, loving every moment, climbing higher and higher.

Her cowboy grabbed hold of her hips and thrust harder and harder into her, moaning with every movement. As one hand continued to massage her breasts, the other circled down around her waist and began to stroke her clitoris. She arched further back into her masseuse, allowing him to start kissing her neck. The two pulled her deeper and deeper into a world of pure bliss, and she moaned every step of the journey. She could feel her cowboy start to tighten underneath her, and she began to feel the beginnings of her own climax. She was so lost in ecstasy that she didn't notice the loss of her masseuse's hands. Then just as her muscles tightened around her cowboy's cock, feeling him explode into her, she felt a rope around her neck. Her own lasso tightened around her throat as she climaxed, but her screams were drowned out by her cowboy's thunderous climax, still raging on underneath her. The rope tightened further, making breathing a very difficult task. She heard a raspy voice from behind her whisper into her ear, "Yee-haw." She felt one final thrust from below as she blew out her last breath of air, and her body fell limp onto the bed.

*

"That's it, Simon." She ran her fingers across the back of his chair as she stepped around behind him. "Just close your eyes and allow yourself to succumb to the moment." She walked her fingertips down his arm as she came around in front of him.

"Feel the rhythm and let your body take over. Forget the world outside this room and just let go." She placed both her hands on either side of him, stared straight into his eyes, and swayed her hips back and forth.

"Don't think before you act. Allow yourself to just flow with the moment." She rolled her body up and down, sliding her hands up his legs as she slid her body upright.

"Feel the sensations and let them drive you! Let them take control! Let them make you want it. Make you need it!" She let her voice drum in his veins, helping his heart beat faster and faster.

"Feel the burning need inside you. Feel yourself stretch and grow from wanting it. Feel yourself pulse with the need for release." She stood, went over to the stereo, and pressed play.

"Feel the tension and the burning desire. Feel the need!" She started to sway to the music.

He watched her body move in time to Webber's "Point of No Return." It was her favorite piece to use when she was in control.

"Go past your own point of no return. Reach for it! Reach for what you want! It's there, so take it!"

He stood up from his seat, grabbed her around the waist, and kissed her fervently.

Chapter 1

She walked out onto the balcony, resting her hands on the railing. Elandra looked around at the street and houses below and took a deep breath. She felt a cool breeze and listened to the gentle sounds of spring—the leaves rustling in the wind and the melodious song of the birds. She smiled as the warm sun heated her skin. She closed her eyes and let her mind take her through her days. It had taken a lot of hard work and time, but she had done it. She had a successful business that continued to grow every day. She was putting all she had learned to good use, making all the years in school worth it. She turned her back on the street and leaned against the railing as she took in the building before her. She worked in the best place possible, and she enjoyed the freedom and versatility of working from home. She even had the added benefit of working with her best friend, as well as a talented staff who were also dear friends. Elandra heaved a satisfied sigh and ventured back inside.

*

He passed by several officers and simply followed the trail of uniforms to the room. He stepped to the door and looked in, pausing one moment to pat an officer on the back as he squeezed through. He looked at the scene that lay before him; a nearly naked woman lay on her back on the bed with a noose around her neck. While the body lay there, cold and decomposing, her eyes were still open, and her face was frozen in a look of sheer horror.

"Her name's Chloe Pattel," an officer said as a way of greeting.

"Let me guess, she's a 'lady of the night,'" he said, adding air quotes.

"No idea. Sass says all the girls are accounted for." The officer replied.

They had an understanding with Madame Sasha: her girls kept it clean. It was simple—the town's best kept secret. Even though everyone knew, they just didn't talk about it. It kept their little town of Birch Cross quiet, comfortable, and happy. The girls were regularly checked, any girl caught doing something illegal was bounced, and the cops ensured the girls' safety. This arrangement made for a city with almost no rapes; dirty laundry was kept legit, and some girls even made it through university without becoming prostitutes. The girls could be strictly placed in jobs: some were bartenders, some confidantes, some dancers, and only the ones who were approved entertained the men's x-rated desires.

"Not one of Sass's girls? You sure, Reilly?" he asked with an air of confusion and disbelief.

"Yeah, ask her yourself if you want. But she says everyone's good," the officer snipped.

"Relax, Reilly! It's just weird, that's all. I'm not doubting or second-guessing you."

The officer shrugged it off. "So far we only know her name, but they're pulling everything they can on her down at the station. She somehow squeezed a wallet into those pants, or whatever you call them."

"Thanks, Reilly."

He walked out of the room and back to his car. He opened the driver side and stood with one foot in the car as he tried to place it all together. He needed the facts, and he needed them fast. They hadn't had anything like this in years—at least not since he'd joined the force. This one case could make or break his career. If they failed, it would rest on him, and he would be busted back down to rookie level so fast it would make his head spin. But if, somehow, they managed to pull it off and catch the bad guy, then it could mean a glowing review and an in for a coveted position with the CIA. As he contemplated what this case really meant to his career, his cell phone rang.

"Kerith here," he stated as he brought it to his ear.

"Okay, here's what we know," an officer at the other end said, shifting papers around. "Her name is Chloe Pattel, twenty-four years old, and she worked at some place called 'Hidden Desires.' Sounds like some kind of porn shop to me." The officer chuckled to himself, "It's new in town and owned by one Elandra Rosedale. She's new, too, so we don't have much on her. Seems like she didn't exist until a few years ago…"

"All right. Any ideas from Sass as to what's going on? She's generally in the know," Kerith asked, sliding his hand down his face, already trying to wipe away the stress.

"Sass doesn't know much. She says some of the girls have been pushed, but who knows? I mean, there are those gangs and such trying to creep down our way from Washington. It could be their way of staking a claim, who knows?"

"Okay, well, give me the address on that Desires place and tell the chief I'm going to check it out."

"Kerith…"

He suddenly recognized the voice on the other end. "Hey, Chief. I was just saying I'm going to check out where that girl worked. If they are trying to come in, then it could be a front."

"Christ." Kerith could hear the stress and anxiety in the old man's voice. "We don't need any sort of mob or gang connections coming in here." He sighed, his voice turning soft. "It's not like Stephanie and Becky, so don't make something out of nothing. I want you to go in, Kerith, but just figure out what the hell is going on—no vigilante crap." He cleared his throat, and his voice became hard again. "I don't like not knowing what's going on in my town."

"Right, Chief." There was a moment of silence. "Don't worry, Chief, we'll stop 'em before they have time to come in." He didn't try to hide the affection and concern in his voice. He had a great bond with the chief; he had been like a second dad ever since he joined the force. He knew the man's love for the city they both called home and felt he owed it to the old man to look after it now that he was tied behind a desk.

"Thanks, Kerith. Hey, you keep this up I might just have to send you away. And it'll be mighty hard to lose ya." The old man cleared his throat, not used to showing emotion. "Well, you get on it. I don't feel like having dead hookers in my town."

"Right, Chief." He chuckled to himself.

Kerith took the information from the officer and fell into his car. It was going to be a long day.

∗

She casually walked into the office and tossed a file folder onto the desk in front of her partner. "Gen, do you have any idea where Chloe is? She missed her appointments yesterday and one this morning already." She picked up the stack of mail and started shuffling through it.

"No clue, El. Haven't heard a word. There were no messages or anything. Sorry hon," the girl at the desk answered, looking up and taking the folder. "Have you tried calling her? Asked Mercedes?"

"There was no answer at home, and Mercedes hasn't heard from her. I'm worried."

"I'm sure it's nothing," Gen replied with a calm tone.

"Initially I'd say that, too, but I got a call from one of her professors this morning." Gen's head shot up in shock, "He told me that she missed a major exam."

Gen frowned, "That's not like her at all. Maybe... maybe you should call the cops or something."

Elandra felt her stomach tighten with fear, "You're right. I was just hoping. You know, I was hoping that maybe it wouldn't have to come to it." She tried to swallow back her fear, "Okay..." She blew out a deep breath. "Can you handle all the calls for a bit, I...I'm going to call them."

"Yeah sure, no problem, hon. You just go and find our Chloe."

5

Elandra walked over and sat down at her desk, taking deep breaths, trying to find her courage with each movement. She pulled the phone across to her and glanced up as Gen silently slipped out of the room, leaving her to make the call on her own. Her shaky fingers absently started dialing, and she closed her eyes, hoping it would make it all disappear. But reality hit her when the phone was picked up.

"Hello, police? I'd like to report a missing person."

Chapter 2

He pulled up to the curb and looked at the scribbled sheet of paper again. This couldn't be right; it was a house, or more correctly, an old Victorian mansion. The place held a certain character, but there was nothing marking that it was a shop of any sort. It just looked like a house: 431 Higben Drive. Nope it was right. He scratched his head, wondering what the hell was going on.

"'Hidden Desires.' What the hell is that?" He shook his head.

He looked up and down the street; a couple of kids playing catch in a yard, a housewife taking out the trash, and a man stopping home for lunch.

"It's a goddamn Stepford!" he cursed silently.

He took a deep breath. Well he was here, and so far it was all they had to go on. He stepped out of the car, slamming the door harder than normal due to his confused state. He slowly sauntered up the path to the house. All the curtains were drawn, and it somehow presented an air of elegant mystery to the quiet neighborhood.

He walked up the steps to the front door. "Well I'll be damned."

Etched on the glass were the words "Hidden Desires." He certainly had the right address. Not sure whether he should ring the bell or just enter, Kerith rubbed his stubble, realizing he had forgotten to shave that morning. *Manners*, Kerith reminded himself. *I mean, hell, an old woman could live here.* He brought his hand up to the doorbell, half expecting some elderly Betty Crocker woman to answer, but paused when he heard voices inside.

"We'll see you next week, Mr. and Mrs. Bryant," came the murmur of a soft voice.

Suddenly the door opened in front of him, and a couple walked out, arm in arm, with giddy smiles plastered on their faces. He grabbed the door before it swung shut. The couple didn't even notice him as they passed by, they were so focused on each other.

"Well come on in, hon," came a voice from behind a desk.

It looked like the entrance to an inn. *Maybe it's a secret getaway for couples.* He absentmindedly walked toward the desk, trying to take in his surroundings.

"You got an appointment, honey, or this your first time?" the voice called to him, snapping him out of his reverie.

"Uh, first time." He managed to sputter out, lost in the atmosphere.

"Okay. Well, my name is Janette." Her voice suddenly took on a sexy French accent. "And welcome to Hidden Desires, where we help you find your inner lover. You'll have to be evaluated by Elandra first, and then you'll be set up with one of our very skilled instructors." She gave him a once over, letting her gaze slowly climb his body. "And I certainly hope that I'll be your teacher." She drew his gaze to her mouth as she suggestively ran her tongue along her lips. "I could certainly teach you how to please a woman, though by the look of you, I'd say that you have a pretty good handle on that."

He cleared his throat, trying to clear his head at the same time. "Um, evaluated?" He tried to sound normal and ease down the beginning of a hard on.

"Yeah. Elandra judges which lessons you're best suited for. Didn't you know that?" Her voice lost its accent and took on a casual tone.

He cleared his throat again. "Um, I'm actually with the police, I'm Detective Kerith Reid. I need to speak with the owner," he said with some semblance of control.

"Cops?" she gulped.

"Yes, and I need to talk to the owner or whoever runs this place," he said, returning to his all-business mindset.

"Well, that would be me," came a sultry voice from the stairs, "It's all right, Jan. I assume you're here about Chloe."

His eyes drifted up to the stairs. She seemed to glide down them, wearing a black skirt that showed off her slender and elegant legs and a form-fitting, knitted V-neck shirt. Her attire allowed her to flip from knockout to business in one step. She ran her hand along the railing as she descended from the second floor. The woman seemed to ooze sex, and Kerith couldn't tear his gaze from her.

She reached the bottom of the stairs and held out her hand for him. "I'm Elandra Rosedale, I own Hidden Desires."

Kerith's mouth was suddenly dry. He gulped back his rising desire and shook her hand. "I'm Detective Kerith Reid."

Elandra felt a jolt of heat race through her at his touch. Their gazes locked for a moment, both silently assessing the other.

She cleared her throat. "Shall we speak someplace private?" She turned and faced the desk. "Jan, honey." She took in the girl's fearful expression. "Don't worry, honey, everything is all right. I'll be back in a bit to take over the desk," she said in a soothing and gentle tone.

The other girl merely nodded in understanding. Elandra led Kerith down the hall and through a set of double doors. They entered into a cozy and elegant living room. Kerith looked around the room, realizing it reflected the exotic woman who had led him there. She sat casually on the couch, and he took the chair opposite.

Kerith took a deep breath and brought his focus back to the reason he was there. "Miss Rosedale, I have a few questions about one Chloe Pattel." He pulled out a notepad and flipped it open.

"Oh, please tell me you found her." She turned into a worried mother in the blink of an eye.

"Found her?"

"Well, yes. I called this morning to report her missing. That is why you're here, isn't it?"

"I wasn't aware you called, but yes, we have found her," he said uncomfortably.

"Oh, thank you. When is she coming home to us?" Elandra asked, her face alight with relief.

"I'm afraid she won't be returning." He paused, unsure how to word it. "I'm afraid she was murdered."

He kept his eyes trained on her to judge her reaction. He watched face flicker with emotion; first pure shock, and then sadness.

"Who would want to hurt Chloe?" She gazed up at him, moisture clouding her vision. "She's only been working here six months, so I don't know her very well."

"Knew." He gave her a look of concern. "You *knew* her."

"What? Oh, yes, I guess so…knew. I didn't know, I mean *knew*, I mean…we weren't well acquainted." Elandra sputtered.

Kerith shifted uncomfortably in his seat, "Well, yes, I know this is a hard time, but I have to ask you a few questions."

He watched her, feeling an odd pain in his chest. He wanted to hug and console her. He'd never had the urge to play rescuer with a woman before. He was entirely lost in his own thoughts, but was brought back to reality by her voice.

"Yes, of course." She fought to regain her composure. "Anything I, or any of the girls, can do to help. You just name it."

Kerith was taken in by her emotion and sincerity; this place might have mob or gang ties, but no matter what it was, this woman was no part of it. He started to chastise himself for jumping to conclusions, but his gut was saying she was clean, and his gut was rarely wrong.

"Well, a few questions were raised with regard to her job. What…um, what…what exactly is it that you do here, Miss Rosedale?" he said, looking around the room, trying to avoid staring at her legs and enjoying the way her skirt shifted up with every movement she made.

Slightly taken aback, Elandra looked at him curiously, "You've never heard of us before?"

He cleared his throat. "Look, so far as I can tell, you run a little burlesque house here in the middle of suburbia," he replied in a sharp, cutting tone.

She took a deep breath, trying to ease her rising anger. "While I do not appreciate your assumption and must state that you are quite rude, I also do not welcome your jumping to conclusions. I can assure you that I do not run a house of *ill-fame*."

"So you don't run a whorehouse?" he asked in a gentle but irritated tone.

Elandra took another deep breath and counted to ten. She felt her face flush with heat. *I did not spend six years at Yale, earn a PhD in psychology, and start my own business to be spoken to in such a manner. What a fucking prick! Composure Elandra, he's a police officer, don't want to fuck this up already.* She took another deep breath and looked up at him. He seemed annoyed that she was taking so long to answer! *The nerve, the…jackass!* She clenched her fists and counted to ten again. *Nope, he still looks like an asshole.*

She let out a large breath and said in her most professional voice, "No, I run a very respectable establishment," she clipped. "While we are not a *whorehouse*, as you call it, we do work with men and the concept of intimacy and pleasure."

"But I've never heard of you," he continued in his crisp manner.

"We find it unnecessary to advertise." She regained her composure—this man was so aggravating.

"So it's a guilty pleasure no one talks about?" he asked, laughing to himself.

"No, detective, it's a school every woman talks about. A school where we teach the shy to take command."

"The shy to take command?" His disbelief seemed to ooze from every pore.

"Yes, wives and girlfriends come to us and tell us about their lackluster husbands or boyfriends. These are men whom they love with all their hearts, but desire a little something more in the bedroom."

"So there's something missing?"

"Yes, it's generally those who have the non-adventurous jobs, like bankers, computer techs, lawyers, and the like."

"And you…what? Teach them to be better lovers?"

"Basically. We assess the men, place them in an environment with the best-suited instructor, and teach them what it's like to give in to deep passion and desire—to want someone so bad you must have them at that very moment," she replied with deep pride and confidence in her business.

He could tell she meant every word she said, for as she spoke, she began to run her left hand up and down her thigh, giving gentle sighs.

"So you teach them how to have sex?" he said with a little chuckle.

"Oh, it's much more than that. We teach these men to feel, to have such a deep seated passion that they have the urge to rip off their clothes and throw their lover back onto the bed and ravage them until…until…." Her breathing had come faster now, her eyes closed in fantasy.

He gulped as he asked the burning question, "Until what?" His voice squeaked.

He cleared his throat, making her open her eyes, and she shot a sly and seductive smile at him. "Until they are both completely sucked dry of that passion and left content."

He started to fidget as he noticed both her hands now sliding along her thighs. He took a handkerchief from his pocket and dabbed at his forehead, which was growing increasingly damp with perspiration.

"And you?" He cleared his throat to eliminate the squeak. "Do you just run the place?"

"Oh no, detective." She slid her legs apart, bringing one up onto the couch and sliding it under her. "I take on our most difficult students."

It was through a combination of the way her skirt was now edging higher up her legs and the way she seductively said "difficult students" that made Kerith grow hard with anticipation for her next movement. He sat there, swallowed by a mind-blowing wave of passion that left him drowning in a sea of need and desire.

Elandra took in the view of Kerith, running her eyes up his long body. Her eyes paused on his obviously chiseled stomach, and then something caught her eye. She noticed the growing bulge straining against his pants, and to avert her eyes, she glanced up and realized his own eyes were pinned on her legs. Though she hated to admit it, she grew warm knowing he was watching her. Watching his eyes, she brought her other leg up and pushed into a full recline. She slowly rolled onto her side, facing her upper body toward him. She watched his eyes grow darker as she slid one leg out and curled the other up a little. Her skirt slid up, right up to the point of no return. His eyes had never left her legs, and he licked his lips while she sat there, thinking of the many things she could do to him. Elandra felt her breath becoming more labored, and she raised her hand to her chest.

Kerith's eyes followed her movement, watching her breasts rise and fall with every breath. He pulled, needing more room in his pants. *Suspect! Suspect! She's a suspect!* his brain yelled at him. *Right. Suspect.*

Kerith took a deep breath and cleared his throat, trying to get a hold of himself. "Um, right, whorehouse…" he sputtered.

Like throwing ice water on a fire, Elandra's growing desire dissolved, and her anger grew again. *Asshole! He still thinks I'm pimping out my girls for prostitution.*

"Look, why are you here, Mister Reid?" Elandra didn't even try to conceal her growing rage.

Aw, shit. He didn't need to piss her off; she was the only one who could help so far. But he had to maintain a professional attitude. He couldn't get involved with a suspect, no matter how tempting her mouth looked. And from the look of her, he was sure she'd taste like sweet honey, and her mouth would fit just perfectly around his…*no!* He couldn't go down that road.

He cleared his throat again, swallowing back the burning desire that was consuming him. "That would be *detective* to you, Miss Rosedale. And I'm here because one of your employees is dead."

"Well her job had nothing to do with it!" Elandra replied incredulously.

"Look, I just want to know what happened. I don't need you to have a hissy fit—"

"Hissy fit? *Hissy fit?*" *Oh he is such an asshole.*

"Yes, a hissy fit." He put his hand up to stop her from interrupting again. "Chloe was found at a motel near the edge of town. Now what's questionable was what she was wearing. She was dressed up like a cowboy with ass-less chaps. She looked like a dressed-up hooker, so that's why I'm here. Now I just need you to answer my questions and be done with it."

"We are not a whorehouse!" she cried. *Breath, Elandra.* She took a deep breath and lowered her voice to normal levels. "If you would like, I can show you around, and you can see exactly what it is we do here."

"Actually, that would be good. And you can explain this so-called teaching you do." He added air quotes.

"Right this way, officer," Elandra said through clenched teeth as she rose from the sofa and led him out of the room.

Chapter 3

Elandra led him down the hall, and with every step she grew more determined. *A whorehouse! Hidden Desires a whorehouse?* She paused mid-step. *Okay, so if you didn't know what it was, then it's easy to confuse it for a brothel.* But that didn't mean she would ever admit it, at least not to this rude and arrogant ass! She marched on; he had no right to berate her pride and joy. She would show him—oh, yes, he would understand what Hidden Desires was really about.

Kerith glanced at the pictures on the wall as they passed. They looked like head shots for actresses. Every face was different, but their black-and-white composition kept them together. He had to admit, each photo held a beautiful girl, each with their own endearing and sensuous traits. He brought his gaze back up to Elandra's retreating figure. Damn! She sashayed and her hips moved just right. He could feel himself growing hard, and he almost started drooling. *Jesus Christ, this woman is delectable. I could just eat her up. No!* A blaring stop sign slammed in his head. *She's a suspect, and who knows, maybe she is involved. She could be playing innocent, it's been done before. I mean she could be playing the sex card on purpose.* No, sex with Elandra was completely out of the question, no matter how much he wanted to wrap his fingers in her hair. *No!* He shook his head to clear it of the vision of Elandra spread before him. He brought his gaze back to focus on Elandra and where she was leading him. But his eyes focused on her slender legs, and he imagined them being wrapped around him. He let out a loud groan just at the thought.

Elandra paused and turned back to him. "What did you say?"

"Oh, uh, nothing," he nervously chuckled.

Elandra shook her head in confusion and turned and faced a door on her left. "Here: command central. If you wish to know about Hidden Desires, then this is where you come."

She opened the door, and Kerith stepped through, Elandra following close behind. Kerith looked around the dim room. It had once been a library, but now it held numerous televisions and controls, much like at a television station. Kerith looked at the screens. Each apparently showed a different room in the house.

"You tape all your customers having sex?" he asked in a biting tone.

"We do not...they don't...ah!" Elandra threw her hands up in anger. She took a deep breath and smoothed her clothes. "Career-driven and powerful women bring their lackluster husbands here. I evaluate their personalities and find where their trigger for passion is likely hidden. I then match them with one of our instructors. Together they work on drawing out the customers' passionate side.

No one wants mechanical sex, so that's where we come in and teach them how to find the excitement in sex. Some benefit from classroom-type lectures." Stepping back into her business stride, she pointed to a screen showing an empty classroom. "They benefit from having it spelled out for them. They were likely the ones who took the best notes in high school. Others just need an insight to their initial arousal. Like here with Jan." She pointed at another monitor.

Kerith directed his attention to the screen. A man was sitting on a large, four-poster bed. The room looked like one from an elegant hotel. Just as Kerith was about to ask what was going on, there was a rap on the door. His eyes glued to the screen, he watched as Jan entered the room. She was wearing a rather short and sassy maid's outfit.

"Oh, excuse *moi*. I did not know anyone was in 'ere." Her voice had resumed the coy French accent.

"Oh. Oh, it's quite all right. I'm just…I'm just waiting for my…my wife," the man stuttered. "Go…go…go ahead and clean if…if you…if you need to."

"*Merci*. My name is Janette, and I'll be out of your way as quickly as I can."

"Watch as Jan pushes his erotic buttons without even going near him," Elandra stated with pride.

Kerith watched as Jan moved to dust off a table and switched to the fireplace. She bent over at the waist, revealing a red and black thong underneath her costume. His eyes glued to Jan's behind, he almost didn't hear Elandra.

"See, Alex is being pushed. He's being turned on just by watching her."

Kerith watched as Jan wiggled her behind, realizing that she must have been taunting her subject as she pretended to clean and dust the fireplace. He then watched her wander toward the bed and bend toward the blankets, showing ample cleavage toward her prey.

"I need you to get up," she said with a coy smirk.

"Um, up?" his voice squeaked.

"I need to make ze bed," she replied, acting casual.

"Oh yes…yes…" he stuttered.

Kerith continued to watch as Jan made a show out of making the bed; she turned, leaned, and wiggled around, drawing great attention to her body.

"This is my favorite part," a man sitting at the controls said as he joined Elandra and Kerith in watching Jan.

They watched as she slithered and glided, the men growing ever increasingly hard with each moment. Just when Kerith thought he could watch no more, Jan rose and left the room, and he watched as another woman entered.

The screen clicked to black. "And that's where his wife takes over," Elandra said in a voice of utmost calm. "The only other type that I have discovered are the ones who need a more hands-on and drawing-out approach; where they physically need the desire pulled out to the surface." Her eyes searched the screens.

"Wow." Kerith drew in a shuddering breath, unsure if he could watch anymore.

"There." She pointed to a screen. "One of our finest instructors. Watch as Gabrielle draws out Matthew's desires."

Kerith focused on the screen. There was a man who stood there all in black, with only a red sash hugging his hips that added a little color. Kerith watched as a woman walked up to the man—and Kerith just stared into the screen, taking in her beauty. She wore a tight, black flamenco dress; the top low-cut and leaving little to the imagination, the skirt flaring out to show the deep red of the underlay, and the long, sensuous legs peeking from within. Her dark curls cascaded down her back, merely graced with a deep red rose tucked behind one ear and kept clearly away from her smoky and sultry eyes.

"See how she first seduces him?" Elandra pointed out.

Kerith watched the screen as the siren took her prey's hand and had him lift her left leg, with her knee to his waist. She took his other hand and placed it on the small of her back. She rolled her upper body in a circle, letting his hand on her back support her weight. She rolled back up, letting her hair sway with the movement before staring deep into his eyes. She flirted with her eyes for a moment, sending shots of desire pulsing through the man's veins.

"Now here is where Gabrielle shines." Elandra beamed proudly. "See how she now draws him into taking the lead."

Gabrielle slid her leg from his hand and placed her hand along his waist. She circled him, dragging her hand along his waist as she did.

"What is it you want, Matthew?" Gabrielle cooed in a sultry Spanish accent. "I am a dancer, I follow your lead."

She circled back around to face him and smiled when he wrapped his arm around her waist and pulled her to him. She turned and pressed her back firmly into his chest, leaving his right arm around her waist. She placed

21

her right arm alongside his and wrapped her left arm up around his neck, leaning back into him. Then she took his left hand and ran it down along the side of her body, sighing as his hand came to rest on her waist.

"I move the way you guide me," Gabrielle urged.

They stood there, frozen for a moment, and then Gabrielle started to swerve her hips to the soft music. Matthew then shifted his left hand, grabbing her right hand, and twirled her around to face him. The screen flicked off just as Matthew pulled Gabrielle closer and pushed his lips against her, swallowing her in a kiss.

"And for students like Matthew, we have a separate room where he joins his wife after he has been drawn into the world of sensuality. His wife waits in that other room, studying what it was that turned him on. She learns what he reacts to, so she can imitate it in their own bedroom," she concluded rather proudly. "So you see, we are not a brothel!" she added with a flare of anger.

"You most certainly aren't," Kerith admitted, his voice squeaking.

Elandra's cheeks flushed as she saw his hungry gaze devouring her. "If, um, if you like, I…I have a class in a few minutes. You could join in and observe if you like."

"You're teaching?" He raised an eyebrow.

"Well, yes, I did start this school." She straightened her back and raised her height a few centimeters.

"Well, I'll be honest, if you were my teacher, I wouldn't be paying attention to the lesson—I'd be daydreaming about you." He chuckled to himself, his voice husky with desire.

"That's the point. We get them revved up, teach them how to take the lead, and send them home to finish the job," Elandra replied in full seriousness.

Kerith swallowed the sudden lump in his throat. "I would absolutely love to join in then. As long as I'm not in the way," he said with a devilish grin.

Elandra looked to the floor and blushed. "No, you wouldn't be in the way at all."

Chapter 4

Elandra led him to the basement, where he found a closed off section with a couple of chalkboards and several desks. The room reminded him of his old elementary classrooms, with a large "teacher's" desk at the front. Kerith checked himself. *This is a case, nothing more. Right…mob, murder, destruction.* He tried to take it all in, but it seemed so surreal. He was supposed to be looking for abuse, drugs, anything that suggested all was not as it seemed. But the fact was, nothing was as he expected, there were no big, muscled men, no dark corners. The place seemed legit. Elandra seemed legit. *The only thing that doesn't fit was this room; it doesn't flow with the others. Maybe the rest really was just the most elaborate front there had been in ages. They said she didn't exist until a few years ago, so maybe she's done this before. Maybe it's this room, with this woman that everything really comes into play.* Kerith raised his eyes and studied Elandra as she smoothly moved toward the large desk at the front.

She motioned toward the rows of desks. "If you'll take a seat, Detective Reid, we'll begin in a few minutes."

Kerith sauntered to the back of the room, taking a seat in the back row so that he could observe it all. He pulled out the chair, watching Elandra's swift movements as she wrote on the board. He stretched his legs out and crossed his arms over his chest. He watched as her clothes clung to her movements, and he felt his body warming in reaction.

"So what do they learn in here, Miss Rosedale? The scientific basics of sex? Do you show them what a penis looks like?" Kerith chuckled. "Or is this a group show of a naughty schoolgirl?"

She turned and faced him, twisting her hair into a bun and securing it with a pencil. "Actually, Detective Reid…" She drew herself upright. "…I happen to have a PhD in psychology, and I've actually developed and reworked some personality tests for my clients."

Kerith cleared his throat, his eyes never moving from Elandra. "You find what turns them on?" he tried to joke, but his laugh faltered when she put on a pair of glasses.

"Actually, yes, and it identifies what their hidden sexual power is. It tells us what kind of teaching they would benefit from, and what triggers deep and intense desire. You see, some actually learn better through visual learning; they learn by taking notes, so we introduce them to a classroom-like setting. Others, like you saw with Alex and Jan, are more auditory, where the underlying messages of what Jan was saying were being read. Generally we start students like that off with reading some passion-filled texts, followed with discussions. Lastly there are those like Matthew, whom you saw with Gabrielle. They're kinetic learners; they learn from doing. We show them what touches and movements to make, and then we let them test it out themselves and see the reactions they elicit." Elandra paused as a few men started to enter the room.

Kerith watched as they came in. Classic nerds—they looked like stereotypical computer geeks. Kerith sat back and surveyed the scene, but his attention was quickly diverted back to Elandra. He examined her completed costume; she looked like a very strict teacher. Elandra started talking and introducing the lecture, but Kerith couldn't focus his mind on her words. *Damn, I am so glad that I didn't have teachers like her.* Kerith's eyes became trained on Elandra's lips, and as he stared, her words slowly started to sink in.

"Women like to know that they are desired, that they can spark a wild lust in someone. Nothing makes a woman feel sexier than knowing she can draw a man to want to just ravish her. Every woman, now and then, wants a man to feel an overwhelming desire for them, a desire so intense that he'll push her back up against the wall and just ravish her because he can't wait to get to the bedroom. Then, once they make it to the bedroom, the unbridled passion continues as he drives into her, and they spend time having wild, hot, sweaty, uninhibited sex." Elandra's voice flowed like honey.

Kerith leaned forward, now intrigued and hanging on her every word. He watched, mesmerized by her every movement. *She's the epitome of power, she defines it, and she helps others find their own kind of power and teaches them how to harness it. She's a woman to be reckoned with, one hell of a woman.*

Elandra's eyes drifted to the back of the room and locked on his confident smirk. *Arrogant ass, let's wipe that smirk off his face.*

"Mister Reid, considering what you seem to know of women, I think it would be wise if you took notes." Elandra's voice chimed in perfect stride with her lesson.

Elandra's own expression formed into a smirk as Kerith's fell into disbelief. She picked up a pen, passing it from palm to palm. She drew in a deep breath and continued with her lesson, "If you all think the notion of romance is dead, if you think this whole thing is silly, then you are sadly mistaken. If you think your wives' complaints are due to the growing feminist movement, then you are mistaken there, as well. For this is an age-old debate, and there have been judges in the times before." She drew a deep breath. Her smirk grew into a large smile, for this was her favorite topic. She raised her head, taking in the students before her, and continued on, "Old Irish lore tells of Aeval, the Fairy Queen of Munster. She possessed the gifts of fairy magic, night magic, prophecy, clairvoyance, freedom, visionary poetry, and spells involving sexual satisfaction. She was a prophet. She predicted the outcome of the Battle of Clontarf with ease and perfection. But her greatest contribution was the justice she served to distressed wives. A great debate once raged in Aeval's Midnight Court. The women of her kingdom found fault with the men, stating that the men were not meeting their sexual needs. The benevolent and fair queen that she was, Aeval listened to both sides state their case. But when all was said and done, Aeval deemed the men guilty. She condemned them as prudes and ordered them to perform as the women demanded.

"You have all been brought here because the women in your lives have charged you with this horrendous crime. Consider me your own personal Fairy Queen, and as it stands, consider yourselves judged guilty." Elandra's eyes ventured up into the group as she surveyed their reaction. She saw the usual fear, concern and...challenge? Kerith was staring at her as if she had just issued a challenge. Elandra felt herself falter, and she fought to pull her gaze away from him. She brought a hand up to her chest and gasped when she saw confidence and desire darken his eyes. Elandra felt heat start to build between her thighs, and the whole room seemed to disappear, leaving just Elandra and him.

Kerith stared deep into her eyes and felt himself being drawn to her. He felt himself getting lost in the energy emanating from her, and his thoughts started to drift to images of Elandra stretched out beneath him. Just as he started to allow himself to enjoy his growing fantasy, a siren went off in his head. *Suspect! Suspect!* Suspect! his mind screamed at him. *Damn, I need to gain control back, I need to throw her off her game.* But before Kerith could even start to think, a voice sounded through the room.

"If you're our personal Fairy Queen, then shouldn't we be serving our sentence?"

Kerith continued to stare up at Elandra's eyes, wondering where the voice came from. Who the hell would be that forward? *If he thinks he's getting his hands on Elandra...he'll have to wait until I'm done with her first.* He watched as a faint blush crept onto Elandra's face. *If I'm ever done with her.*

Suddenly he realized where the voice was coming from as it spoke again. "Well, your highness..." His hand went to his throat as he realized the words were coming from him.

Elandra's world seemed to shake like an earthquake. Well, that was a challenge if ever she heard one. She swallowed the lump she suddenly realized was in her throat. *The man is an ass. He thought we were a whorehouse,* Elandra's conscience called to her. *Come on, who's really teaching this class? It's time I show him what seduction really means.*

Elandra straightened her shoulders. "Actually, Mister Reid, let me show you your sentence. We're going to have a little demonstration, and Mister Reid has just kindly volunteered his aid. If you would join me up front, please." Elandra allowed her eyes to lower, and she gave a mischievous smirk at Kerith's apparent shock.

It was Kerith's turn to look flustered. He cleared his throat and slowly rose from his seat, dragging himself to the front of the room.

"If you could bring that couch over to the front here, Reid," Elandra instructed as she pointed toward an elegant chaise.

Kerith gently dragged it over, placed it beside the desk, and stood before it beside Elandra.

"I want you to face me and place your left hand on my waist," she instructed. "I'm going to show you all how the women in your lives wish you desired them. I'm going to show you the kind of intensity they crave."

Kerith's head jerked up, and he gazed into her eyes.

"Are you afraid, Mister Reid?" Elandra toyed.

"Hardly." Kerith fought to try to maintain power.

Kerith walked forward and placed his hand on her waist, and instantly he felt a jolt of electricity shoot through his veins. He felt like his blood was on fire—he'd never reacted this intensely before. He fought the urge to grab her to him and kiss her with all he had. She was what he wanted. He hadn't felt desire like this rip through him since Stephanie. Stephanie, his beloved Stephanie…Kerith's mind started to drift into the past, but was brought sharply back to the present by a small sigh that had escaped Elandra's lips. Kerith's whole body went rigid in response.

The simple touch on her skin sent shots of passion and fire through her. She knew this was it; she knew now what intense and true desire felt like. She wanted him like she had never wanted any man before. She angled her face toward him, reaching for him, needing him to touch her, to feel her, to consume her. *This is insane, this man is an ass. I should not be reacting this way. If I keep telling myself I'm not attracted to him, then I won't be.* She looked up into his eyes. *Yeah right.* He swept a strand of hair behind her ear, and she melted at his touch. He slid his hand down her cheek and let it follow across her jaw-line. He reclaimed his hand, making her whimper at the loss of his touch.

He took a step back, realizing that he was flirting with disaster; he was so close to just taking her. It was hard for him not to touch her, for he could see in her eyes and feel in her skin how much she wanted him. He glanced down into her eyes and felt his own passion enflame, and he could feel himself straining against his jeans. He stared at her for a moment and then decided to give in to his desire, but found himself frozen. What was happening? He obviously wanted her—the bulge in his pants confirmed it—but why couldn't he just take her?

He had never had trouble taking command when it came to affairs of the bedroom. But now he just stood there, frozen, wanting the world to collapse if he couldn't reach out and touch her.

She trained men to take control in the world of passion. It was her job. So she should want him to take control and let him pull her into his imaginative world of bliss. But as she stood there, mere inches from his hard body, she could only fight the urge to be dominant. She wanted nothing more than to be in control, to push him on the chaise and have her way with him.

Elandra's world shook with the force of an earthquake as words from the world outside of her and Kerith sunk in.

"Umm, Miss Rosedale?"

"What? Oh, yes, what can I do for you, Reggie?" Elandra shook the cobwebs from her clouded mind and faced the room.

"It's time to go."

"Go? But…" Elandra felt like a bucket of ice had been thrown in her face. "Yes, go." Elandra shook herself back to reality, "We're done here, you can all go."

Kerith leaned forward and gently grabbed Elandra's left hand, causing her to turn and face him. "Elandra…"

Elandra quickly drew her hand back. "It's time you go, Mister Reid, I have many things to do here." She turned and did everything to avoid looking at him.

Kerith hesitated a moment. *What did I do wrong? Give her space, you know she felt it too, she had to. Give her space.* "All right. Well, if you can gather any information you have on Chloe to help us figure out who her company was, that would speed things along."

Chloe...right, he was here about Chloe. Poor Chloe... "Yes of course." Elandra busied her hands shuffling papers on her desk.

She glanced up just in time to see him pass through the door. *Chloe...*

Chapter 5

Elandra wandered into the office, quietly closing the door behind her. "Gen, can you find me Chloe's address?"

"No problem, El. What's up?" Gen asked.

"I'm going to head over to Chloe's. Something isn't sitting right with me." She started rifling though papers at her desk.

"What do you think you'll find? A note saying 'so and so killed me'?" Gen joked.

"So you heard?"

"Yeah…" Gen's voice drifted off. "It was bound to happen."

"What? What the hell does that mean? Are you saying Chloe was bound to be murdered?" Elandra raged.

"What? El, no. I…I mean we were all gonna find out sooner or later. I mean, a hot cop comes to talk to you about Chloe. Once Gerry told me you took him to the control room, then, like any good best friend, I spied on you guys in the classroom. El, hon, I never meant anything against Chloe."

Elandra heaved out a sigh. "I know. I'm sorry, sweetie, I just…who would want to hurt our Chloe?"

"I don't know. What do you think you'll find at Chloe's?"

"I don't really know." She glanced back at Gen. "But she never kept anything here, maybe I can find something at her place saying where she was."

"Like whether she was meeting someone somewhere and stuff like that?"

"Yeah, something like that."

"I don't know El; I don't think you should be playing Nancy Drew." Gen looked at her with concern. "Chloe's dead, and someone killed her. Don't you think we should leave it to the cops to figure out what happened?"

"Well, Reid said that any information on Chloe, where she relaxes and all that, I should pass it on. So I see this as working for the police; he did ask me to gather and pass on information. I'm simply doing them a favor." She smiled, trying to ease Gen's tension.

"Reid, eh? You be careful, El. Getting involved with cops can be dangerous to your heart."

"I don't know what you're talking about." Elandra avoided Gen's gaze and smiled at the ground.

"That's what I thought." Gen smirked and walked over to Elandra. "Here." She handed her a slip of paper. "Go play Nancy Drew."

"Thanks, I'll give you a call and fill you in."

"You better!" Gen grinned.

Elandra started to walk toward the door.

"El?"

"Yeah?" Elandra's hand froze on the doorknob as she turned and faced Gen.

"It's good to see you happy. I haven't seen that smile in a long time. Just be careful."

"Always." Elandra smiled and walked out.

*

Elandra walked up to the door, and looked at the roster call at the left side of the entryway. She rolled her finger down the list, found Chloe, and pressed the buzzer of the one above.

"Yes?" came a timid little voice.

"Hi, I'm a friend of Chloe's. She asked me to come by and pick up something for her dad, and said to just stop by. But I called up, and she's not answering. I was wondering if you could let me in. She told me that if she wasn't here to just come on up anyways, but I just realized that she forgot to leave me her key. So if you could help me out, that would be great." Elandra held her breath, praying that her meek excuse would work.

There was a pause of silence, and then the voice returned. "No problem, dearie. I've got a spare key, that girl never could remember very much. I'll be right down."

The door clicked open, and Elandra stepped in from the cold breeze. She waited but two minutes, and a slight figure descended the stairs. Elandra took in the image of the little elderly woman, noticing the slight hump in her back and the brown knit sweater she wore. Elandra quickly stepped forward and helped the woman down the last step.

"Now you're the friend of Chloe's, right?" the woman asked.

"That would be me." Elandra smiled. "So sorry to bother you."

"Oh, no worries, dearie. My sweet Chloe never could remember things. In fact, she gave me a spare key after she forgot her own key a number of times and I had to let her in. I've taken to looking after her like she was my own granddaughter. My girls live way out West so she's the closest I've got." She answered with a spark of affection.

"Well thank you so much for letting me in." the pair turned and started up the stairs again.

"No problem. Now, I haven't seen Chloe for the past few days, but I assume that she's gone to Washington to talk to that mother of hers. They don't get along at all, but she called last week. So I assume Chloe's off to see her," the woman stated.

"Her mother called?" Elandra asked, having remembered that Chloe had told her that her mother was dead.

"Yes. That woman refuses to talk to Chloe's father, so she uses Chloe to get money from him." She walked Elandra to the door of 2B. "Her parents divorced a while ago, and her mother just wants the money." She made an angry face that Elandra couldn't help but laugh at. "Now I'm just across the hall." She opened the door. "So if you need anything, just holler. My name is Elizabeth, but everyone calls me Liz." She smiled. "I hope you get everything, Lord knows my Chloe wasn't the neatest."

"Well thank you again, Liz," Elandra stated, watching as she turned back into her apartment.

Elandra stepped in and closed the door behind her. She turned around and froze. *Holy crap! Liz wasn't kidding, I knew Chloe wasn't the most organized, but jeez.* Elandra carefully picked her way across the room through the piles of clothes strewn about the floor. She stopped at the couch and bent down, picking up a notebook. Human Interactions; it had been Chloe's favorite course, and she was supposed to graduate next year. *What happened to you, Chloe? You had such plans, and we planned everything out.* She stood back up and carried the book with her to the kitchen, where she dropped it on the counter. *Who were you with, Chloe?* She wandered up to the answering machine. Three messages. Elandra pressed play.

"Hey, Chloe, it's Isaac from Human Interactions. I was hoping I could borrow your notes before the midterm. I mean yours are so much better than mine. We could get coffee or something. Anyways, you know the number, so call me, and we'll get together."

"Chloe, It's your mother; I need you to talk to that man that is my ex-husband. He is impossible! He's threatened to cut my allowance again. So you have to talk to him and do it soon, I want to go to Paris when congress takes a break."

"Hey, sweetie, I left the directions for you with Gen. Believe me, honey, you will have a lot of fun with Victor—a lot of fun. Anyways, let me know how it goes. Talk to you later."

Elandra recognized the last voice as her employee, Mercedes. "Victor? Who would Mercedes be introducing you to, Chloe?" Elandra asked the room.

Elandra wandered around, running a hand along the wall, trying to get a feel for Chloe. *Okay, if I'm going to find anything in here I have to start thinking like Chloe. So how do I do that?* Elandra came upon a crowded bookcase and found Chloe's stereo. *When in doubt, follow the music.* Elandra smiled to herself as she turned it on. She closed her eyes and let herself feel the music. *Carlos Santana, just like my Chloe.* Elandra felt herself start to move to the music, and she opened her eyes. She walked through the room and down the hall. She opened the hall closet and peeked in—nothing. She continued on down the hall and into the bedroom, where she walked up to the bed and ran her hand over the sheets. Her hand hit something hard, and she pulled back the blankets. Chloe's laptop, of course. *Doesn't every girl sleep with her laptop?* Elandra laughed. She flipped it open and turned it on: password protected. *Goddamnit, Chloe. You'll throw everything else around but you'll protect people from using your laptop?* Elandra let out a frustrated sigh and wandered over to the large armoire and pulled back the doors.

She was immediately assaulted by falling clothes knocking her to the ground. "Ah! Fumphade!" she muffled through the clothes. She pulled a sweater and shirt off her head. "Holy shit, Chloe, enough clothes?" She picked up something black. "And what the hell is this? Is it...ew! It's, like, plastic and has chains, ack!" She threw it to the side.

Elandra picked herself up and stared inside, and her hands floated over the few hangers. She noticed something behind them and quickly pushed them to the side. *A bulletin board? What in the world is it doing in her closet? Wait a minute...*

"Monday, Kyle Winslow = Cowgirl; Wednesday, Graham Morris = Chef; Thursday, CLASS..." *It's her schedule, she'd have to look at it everyday when she opens her closet! Well I must say Chloe, I'm impressed, that's a really smart idea.* Elandra smiled. *That's my girl. Okay, who did you meet Saturday, Chloe?* Elandra ran her finger along the roughly hand drawn calendar. *Saturday...*

"Saturday, Highway Motel = Victor Prescott."

"Prescott? That sounds familiar. Hmm…well, it's Victor, so it must be who Mercedes was talking about." Elandra turned back into the room thinking aloud, "Prescott…Prescott…wait a minute."

She quickly ran back out to the living room and pressed the play button on the answering machine again. She listened to the messages again, waiting for Mercedes's voice.

"Victor…Victor Prescott…" Elandra groaned as everything clicked into place. "Mercedes trained Victor Prescott. He was the odd one." She jogged her memory. "He was the politician. Yeah, the senator, that's right. The senator…oh." Her voice dropped along with her heart. "The senator. Mercedes set up a meeting…oh, Chloe, what did you get yourself into?" she sighed.

Elandra wandered back over to the stereo and shut it off. She leaned on the shelves for support as she felt her heart break for Chloe. Her head swirled in a sea of confusion, pain, and sadness; she felt her eyes grow watery. She sniffed back the tears and looked up, trying to compose herself. That was when she saw it: a photograph on its own little shelf, kept perfectly neat. Elandra picked up the photo, recognizing the two women in it. She ran her hand over the frozen form of a smiling Chloe hugging an overjoyed Liz. Elandra sighed as she carried it with her to the door; she opened the door and turned to stare back into the apartment. She drew a deep breath, turned, and walked out into the hall. She wandered to the door across the hall and knocked.

"Coming," came the voice from inside.

Someone has to tell her—but not until we know what happened, then Reid can tell her. She sighed as the door opened. "I'm all done, Liz, and I couldn't find anything in that mess, but I'm sure Chloe won't miss it." She tried hard to smile. "Here." She handed Liz the photo. "Chloe told me to give it to you."

"Oh, that's so sweet. Chloe knows that I lost my copy of that picture when my apartment got broken into a while ago. That's my favorite photo of her; she came over to have Thanksgiving dinner with me when my granddaughters couldn't make it." Liz smiled, remembering.

"Well I have to go, but thank you again for letting me in, Liz."

"Oh, it's no problem, dearie." Liz smiled as she waved good-bye.

Elandra walked down the stairs and out the front door, stopping on the stoop and digging out her cell phone.

"Hey, El, what'd you find out?"

"Gen can you meet me at the Red Dragon?"

"Sure, El, but why not the house?" Gen asked hesitantly.

"'Cause I need a clear head, free of work stuff. And besides, what I found can only be discussed over a drink. A very strong drink at that."

Chapter 6

*E*landra waited nervously for Genevieve as she sat in the booth, running her fingers around her glass. Her mind raced with her newfound knowledge: Chloe; Victor Prescott; Mercedes; the senator; the motel…Elandra's mind swam, and she didn't even hear the approaching footsteps.

"This is for you." Elandra fell back to reality as the clink of a glass hit the table. "The gentleman in the booth at the far corner sent it over." The waitress stated.

"Oh." Elandra directed her gaze and stared into the darkness of the other booth.

The light had been dimmed so much that she couldn't make out her benefactor's face. She raised the glass in appreciation and took a careful sip. Her nerves rattled as she sat in confusion and shock. What is going on in my house? Elandra's mind swam once more, but she shook herself from her reverie as she heard someone approach.

"El?" Gen's voice was a sweet welcome in Elandra's confused world.

"Hey." She gave a sigh of relief as Gen slid into the seat across from her.

"So what'd you find that requires…wait, what is that?" Gen asked with a slight smirk, looking at Elandra's drink.

"Oh, well I don't know actually, a guy sent it over." Elandra's voice shook a little as she spoke.

Genevieve looked at Elandra with concern. "Okay, hon, out with it. What'd you find out?"

Elandra took a deep breath and started, "Chloe had a meeting set up with one of our clients outside of the house."

"Ok so, that's a bit of a problem, but why does it sound like the end of the world?"

"Well, first, it was set up by Mercedes. Chloe didn't even set it up herself, so it makes me wonder what Mercedes is doing outside of work."

"That's true." Gen mulled it over for a moment, "Mercedes working outside with our clients is a bad thing. But that still doesn't explain the need for a drink."

"Well," Elandra drew a deep breath, trying to regain her composure, "the one Chloe was set up to meet…"

"Yeah?"

Elandra leaned forward, signaling Gen to lean in. "It was Senator Prescott," she whispered.

Gen bolted straight up in her seat, "*What?*"

"Shh…" Elandra hushed, looking around the room.

Gen leaned in once more. "Sorry. You mean that Chloe was supposed to meet with Senator Prescott?"

"Yeah, and it gets worse."

"Worse?" Gen's voice turned into a high-pitched whisper.

"They were supposed to meet at a motel." Elandra sat back, letting Gen take it all in.

Gen also sat back, her mouth open in shock. "Now I need a drink." She signaled the waitress. "Can I get a Lemon Drop cocktail please?"

"Make it two," Elandra added.

Gen took a deep breath, letting it all sink in, "All right, let's see, we've got Mercedes arranging something behind our backs with our clients. Chloe was supposed to meet the senator, one of our biggest hush-hush clients. And to top it all off, she was supposed to meet him at a motel, which is where they found her."

Elandra nodded her head in agreement. "Yup, that's about the sum of our problems."

"Okay. Mercedes; we'll just ask her. We'll have to talk to our lawyer about something stricter for our privacy agreement with the girls. And, well, we can't exactly do anything about Chloe having met with him now, so we have to let that one go." Gen stated.

"We don't have any proof that she did meet with him, though."

"True, but either way, we can't do anything about it now."

Elandra let out a deep sigh. "You're right." She put her head in her hands. "What are we going to do, Gen? What if the girls are working behind our backs?"

Gen sighed in response. "I don't know, El, but I don't think we're going to figure any of it out tonight."

"Once more, you're right." Elandra raised her head and played with her glass. "I say we sleep on it and get a fresh start tomorrow."

"Sounds like a plan to me. I'll see you first thing at the house." Gen raised her glass. "Here's to finding out the truth."

"Cheers." Elandra raised her glass in response, and they finished them off.

The girls placed money on the table and rose. "It'll all be okay, El," Gen added.

"I know, I just wish none of it were happening."

They sighed in unison and started to walk to the door. "I gotta use the bathroom, but I'll see you tomorrow morning."

"Bye, hon." the girls hugged and parted ways.

Chapter 7

"Well, hello there, sweet thing," a deep voice chimed.

Elandra looked to her right as she passed through the door. Shrouded in shadows, the street lamp clearly showed the silhouette of a tall man leaning against the wall.

"You need an escort, honey?" the timbre voice echoed through the night. He pushed himself off the wall and placed his hands in his back pockets.

"No, thank you. I'm quite capable of handling myself, thank you very much," Elandra stated with a nervous confidence.

"Oh, I don't doubt that." He ran his gaze up and down her body.

Elandra clutched her purse tighter to her, feeling her entire body stiffen. "No, I really am all right, thank you," she stated, her fear starting to creep into her voice.

"That's all right, I was just offering. Just trying to do my good deed for the day. No need to get your panties in a twist, honey." He put his hands up in surrender.

"My panties are not…they're not in a…my…my…my panties are none of your business." She turned, shocked and stuttering.

"Sorry, I didn't mean to make you nervous. And you're right, your panties are none of my business." He chuckled, "Though I would like to get to know them a little better."

Elandra took in a short gasp of air. "Oh, my."

"I saw you in there, and I just couldn't screw up the courage to talk to you inside. And I thought if I could approach you on your own…" he chuckled and ran a hand through his hair.

Elandra allowed herself to laugh a little, and the tension in her shoulders melted away. *It's amazing, despite teaching countless men about passion, I've experienced so little of it in my own life.*

"I had originally wanted to ask you to coffee, but considering how I scared you, I'd settle for simply walking you home or to your car, ensuring your safety." He laughed and dug his hands back into his pockets.

A warm feeling crept through Elandra's body, and she smiled, looking into the shadows that still surrounded him. "Well…"

"Aw, please. I'll get down on bended knee if you really want me to," he chuckled.

Elandra allowed herself to let out a laugh. *Come on, allow yourself to feel the passion for a change.*

"You have a beautiful laugh." His voice was like honey.

"Maybe a knight in shining armor is all right every once in a while," she replied, tucking a few strands of hair behind her ear.

"Whew." He breathed out and chuckled, "Would you think it dorky of me if I did a little happy dance now?"

Elandra allowed herself to laugh again and felt her remaining tension fall away. He held his hand out, urging her to lead the way.

"I just have to get to my car, which is parked in a lot a couple blocks away, but I must say it is nice to know that I won't be alone."

He walked beside her, but somehow managed to stay hidden by the shadows. *My dark hero*, she thought; she didn't mind him staying in the shadows that much, because it allowed her to believe that he was whatever she wanted. Just having someone walk with her in the otherwise pitch black night was comforting.

They walked together in silence for a while and turned on to an empty road. The threat of the storm had driven everyone inside, which left Elandra and her companion alone, the sound of their footsteps echoing through the silence. As they came upon a small alley in between buildings, she felt his fingers graze her arm. Elandra turned around to see what he wanted when her body was pulled into the alley and slammed up against the brick side of a building.

"What the—" Elandra gasped out as pain sprang through her back.

He held a tight grip on her arms, pinning her to the wall. Elandra tried to push back. He moved his head in and sniffed in her scent, "Mmm…you smell good."

"Get off of me!" Elandra cried, trying to push him away with her hands, her upper arms still pinned to the wall.

"Aw, come on, honey." He leaned in and kissed her neck, "I just want to get reacquainted."

"What the hell..." Elandra continued to struggle, "...are you talking about? I don't know you!"

He kissed his way up her neck. "Ah, but you do, sweet thing." He kissed down her jaw line, "You do." He continued to kiss her face, but avoided her lips. "You still have my mark, my little firecracker."

Elandra suddenly froze. No had one had called her firecracker in a long time. No one but...

"Oh, my god!" she gasped out in sheer horror.

He bent his head down, pulling down the neck of her shirt and bra, revealing the top of her breast. "That's right, darling, I'm back. I told you I'd find you again."

He leaned his head down and kissed a small scar on Elandra's breast; it seemed to burn under his lips.

"Oh, yes. You may have changed your name, even changed your appearance, but you still taste the same, Cassidy." He moved his head back up and met her gaze, "And I found you again."

He took Elandra's arms and raised them above her head, locking them in place with just one hand. "Oh, god! Please, no..." she begged.

He ran his other hand down her body, encircling her waist. "Oh, yes, and it's going to be like old times." He kissed up her neck. "Just like old times."

Elandra tried to squirm her way out of his grip, but it only made him tighten it further. He looked up into her eyes. Her tears threatened to fall, but Elandra wouldn't let him see that he was getting to her.

"Oh, I've had lots of playmates in the last few years, Cassidy, but you're still my favorite. I just loved the way you withered underneath me when you came."

Fear now gripped Elandra's heart, and unshed tears stung her eyes.

"We're going to have fun, like the old times, Cassidy. And we're going to start right..." His hand circled farther down her stomach. "...now."

Elandra gasped as he plunged his finger deep into her core, the shock making her body slam further into the wall.

He pulled his finger slightly out. "Remember how good I made you feel?" He brought his face within inches of hers. "I want to make you come again, Cassidy." He whispered a kiss to her cheek. "Come for me babe. Come for me hard." He whispered into her ear as he drove his finger back in.

Elandra couldn't fight anymore. She let the tears fall down her face as her whole body jerked in orgasm. Just as he had, so many years ago, he found her G-spot without trial.

"That's it, Cassidy, let it rip through you."

Elandra moaned and cried as she rode out her orgasm, her body slowly shuddering to a stop. He let go of her hands, and she fell into him with all her weight. Her legs felt like Jell-O, and though her body felt at ease, she was still struck with terror.

He reached down and undid his belt. "Oh, yeah, baby, just like I remember it." He lowered his pants, revealing his large and hardened cock.

No, I'm not letting him do this to me again.

He grabbed his cock in one hand. "Now it's my turn, honey."

Elandra didn't have time to think through her next step; she simply felt her body take control. She took advantage of his uneven stance, knowing he wouldn't be able to chase after her. Her arm flew out and punched him, breaking his nose, and she kicked him as he reeled back in pain. She clutched her purse and coat close to her and took off running. The rain suddenly started to pelt down around her. Elandra ran down the street, losing track of where she was. As she ran on, she dropped her purse, but refused even to look back as she continued on.

She quickly turned the corner, grabbing her coat close to her as she tried to shield herself from the rain. She never looked back, she just kept running. How could this be happening? She had no idea where she was going, but she wasn't about to stop. The rain poured down on her as she ran, outdone only by the tears now streaming down her face. Elandra raced down the road, fighting back her tears as she clung her coat tight to her chest. As she started to cross a road, she skidded to a stop, just missing an oncoming car. Her right heel broke as she fought to maintain her balance. She scrambled up to the curb and fell onto the sidewalk. She fought to maintain herself as she pulled herself up and took off her shoe. She sniffed, trying to hold the tears at bay. She stumbled across the sidewalk and leaned back against the nearest building. She let go of her coat and brushed her wet hair off her face. She leaned her head back and let the rain cascade down her face as her tears joined the steady streams. She suddenly felt very exposed and fisted her hand in her coat, closing herself off to the elements. She sobbed as the rain poured down and closed her eyes, allowing her emotions to take full hold.

Suddenly Elandra's eyes flew open as she heard the pounding of feet heading in her direction. She squinted her eyes against the darkness and fought to see a figure heading toward her through the sheets of rain. She gasped as her body bolted forward from the wall, making her stiff as a board. She stared into the darkness and rain as she tried to determine if the figure was still advancing. With a flash of lightning she saw the strong, large form of a man running toward her. Elandra's heart started to race, and before she knew it she was running down the street, the rain pounding against her. She clutched her coat even more tightly closed—as if it would protect her—and unconsciously cemented her grip on her shoe. She could hear the pounding footsteps behind her, as steady as the rain. The lightning lit her twists and turns, but soon her tears won out, making it impossible to see. She sobbed as she tried to run harder, the footsteps fast approaching. She ran with all her might, fearing that if she stopped, it would be the end.

It's not supposed to end this way.

She kept sobbing, though it felt as though she had run out of tears. Just then, her remaining heel caught in a crack in the sidewalk, and she crashed down to the ground. She screwed her eyes shut as she made impact, her heel in her hand hitting her below the eye. The world seemed to stop as she pulled herself to her knees, unable to move. Suddenly, the sound of the rain muted as she heard the footsteps barreling toward her. Her mind snapped into place.

No, this is not how it's supposed to end!

Her breath shaking, Elandra fisted her hands. She would not go down without a fight! She drew a deep breath and raised herself to her feet. She started to run, but her left ankle gave out. As she started to fall, someone grabbed her from behind. She beat her hands against the arms around her waist.

"Let go of me!" she yelled as she continued to beat the arms that held her.

Consumed by fear, anger, and survival instincts, she didn't hear him calling to her. It wasn't until her heel smashed into his arm, and he yelped in pain that she connected back with the real world. Realizing she had a weapon, she pounded her heel into his, as yet, unyielding arms. With one final blow, he yelped in pain and released his grip, letting her fall to the pavement. She crashed with a thud, realizing the shooting pain in her ankle meant that she could no longer run. Planning on fighting off her pursuer with her shoe, Elandra glanced up into the pelting rain with fire in her eyes.

"Jesus, woman, what the hell was that for?" she heard a voice call through the rain.

Her shoe poised at the ready for a fight, she squinted into the darkness. A flash of lightning revealed her pursuer rubbing his arm in pain.

"Goddamnit, Elandra, what the hell happened?"

"Kerith?" she asked, confused, faintly recognizing his voice.

He knelt down beside her, still rubbing his arm. Nearby, a streetlight flickered to life, enveloping them. Now able to see her through the rain, he raked his eyes over her body, taking in her disheveled look. He abandoned his arm to brush her soaked hair from her face.

"What the hell happened to you?" His voice took on a concerned tone.

She looked up into his eyes and fell apart. She leaned against him, wrapping her arms to her body, burying her face in his shoulder as she cried. He hugged her tight and stroked her head.

"Shh...it's all right. No one's going to hurt you," he said as he held her protectively.

She sobbed into his shoulder for a few minutes, trying to let the rain wash away her fear and pain. They found a forgiving cab and settled their soaked bodies into the backseat as it whisked them off into the night.

Chapter 8

The door slid open, allowing the dim light from the hallway to seep in. Kerith took two steps inside, threw his keys on the side table, and showed Elandra in.

"You should stay here tonight, you'll be safe."

Elandra slid her way into the apartment, clutching her coat tightly and pushing the wet hair back away from her forehead. She stopped in the hallway and hesitantly stood, glancing around the apartment.

"I really should get back to the house," she muttered in a hoarse whisper.

"You can't, they'll probably be waiting there for you. They'll want to finish what they started," Kerith firmly but calmly said.

Elandra's face took on an expression of sheer terror. "Oh," was all she was able to say.

Kerith's heart kicked back at him. "Sorry. Ah, Jesus, I didn't mean to sound so harsh. I just…" He ran his hand through his hair and took a deep breath. "I just think it's best if you stay here with me tonight. There's no way they could have followed us, so you'll be safe here."

"Okay," she replied meekly.

It hurt Kerith to see her this way. She was normally so vibrant, and that was one of the things that attracted him, and now…now she just looked plain scared.

"Um, the spare bedroom is just through here, first door on the right. Well, I guess it has to be the right, I mean it's just a wall on the left so…" He nervously laughed.

"Thank you."

Elandra still clung her clothes tightly to her, and Kerith simply looked at the floor, unsure what to do next.

"Um, do you have anything I could wear?"

His head jerked up. "What?" his voice squeaked.

"These clothes are soaked, and I need to get changed," Elandra said calmly.

"Right. Yes, I need to get you out of those clothes." He took a step toward her and then stopped, realizing what he had said. "I mean, oh, jeez."

Elandra giggled quietly to herself—she liked seeing him nervous.

"Um, I mean, I have some clothes; here, let me go get them." He headed off down the hall.

Elandra looked around the apartment, cheering silently to herself when she noticed no pictures of possible girlfriends. *Oh, come on, now is not the time. You were just attacked, he's only being nice. Besides he probably still thinks we're a whorehouse. He's a jackass and so you should not be attracted to him. But he looks so…*Elandra's mind froze as she realized that she really was attracted to him.

"Um, are sweatpants and an old T-shirt of mine okay?" he called from down the hall.

"Yeah, anything will do."

She slowly walked down the hall and entered the spare room. *You will not be attracted to him, you will just stop it right now.*

"Um, Elandra?" he called.

"In the spare room," she called back to him. *Not attracted…not attracted…*

Kerith stood outside the door, took a deep breath, and walked in, clothes in hand.

"Sweet Jesus," he gasped, stopping dead in his tracks.

Elandra had her back to him. She had thrown her coat on the nearby chair and was presently bending over, in the process of peeling off her soaked skirt. Kerith stared for a moment, taking in and making a mental picture of the moment. He then diverted his gaze to the ground and cleared his throat, holding out the clothes for her.

"Oh!" She gave a startled gasp. "Um, thanks." She took the clothes and quickly threw on the sweatpants.

"Um, let me go get something for your cuts." Kerith quickly excused himself from the room.

Elandra sat down on the bed and started to lift her shirt, but doubled over in pain, clutching her side. Kerith heard her yelp of pain and was on the bed by her side in a flash.

"Here, let me help." He leaned forward, lifting the edge of her shirt slightly.

Elandra grabbed his hands, stopping him, and drew in a sharp breath, feeling electricity shoot through her veins. *This isn't the time to get turned on.*

"You're hurt; you can't do this by yourself," Kerith tried to reason with her, at the same time fight his overwhelming desire to simply rip off her shirt.

Elandra merely nodded her agreement and slightly lifted her arms.

Take it easy now, boy, she's been hurt. He wanted to pull her in his arms and protect her from the world, and he wanted that about as much as he wanted to just throw her back on the bed and have his way with her. He took a deep breath and slowly started to peel her shirt up her torso. She flinched only when she had to raise her arms above her head, but Kerith's smooth and gentle touch eased her pain. Elandra drew in quick gasps of breath as Kerith's touch continued to electrify her. He gingerly eased her shirt over her head, tossed it off to the side, and ran his fingers back down her bare arms.

He ran his hands back up, carefully sliding off the straps of her bra, and tracing his fingers down the front of her chest, he felt her breasts rise and fall with every breath she took. He pulled down the smooth, rose lace, revealing the curve of her left breast. As he was about to taste the sweet nectar in front of him he paused. There was a small scar at the top of her breast that had remained hidden by her clothing. He ran his finger over it, and she grabbed his hand.

"A reminder of a life long passed," she whispered, turning her head to the side. *I shouldn't be doing this.*

He lifted her chin and gazed into her eyes as they grew darker every moment with desire—but he also saw the hint of pain she was trying to hide. He told himself that, in time, she would tell him; that he would hear the story behind the burn she concealed. But now...now was the time for passion. He licked his lips and watched her gasp before he lowered his head and gently kissed the spot that caused her great pain.

He kissed his way up her neck, around her cheek, and down to her chin, stopping before he reached her lips. Their heads rested against each other for a minute, and he listened to her deep and heavy breathing.

Elandra's mind called out to her, *Do it! For once let yourself feel the passion.* She opened her eyes and felt all her doubts melt away as she gazed into his dark eyes. He brought his hand up and cupped her cheek, running his finger against her smooth skin. She flinched when his touch glided over where she'd been hit as she fell. She grabbed his hand and brought it to her mouth kissing it with little butterfly kisses. His eyes darkened, and he let out a moan as she sucked a finger into her mouth, massaging it with her lips and tongue. She savored the taste of him, moaning as she imagined what else they could do. He pulled back his hand and tilted her gaze up to meet his; their eyes connected, and they both felt the flicker of a flame start to burn inside each of them. He cupped her face and swallowed her in a kiss. His hand slid down her back and caressed her butt, pulling her closer to him. She pressed her hands to his chest, loving the feel of the power emanating from him. She felt herself getting absorbed in his touch, and she deepened the kiss further. He was the first to break, suddenly finding he needed some air. Elandra gave a little sigh of pleasure as they caught their breath. Kerith felt such a strong pull to this woman—there was something, he wasn't sure what, but he found that it was like he couldn't look away from her. He wanted to possess her; he wanted to please her.

He slid his hands down her arms and released the clasp of her bra, letting it fall to the floor.

"Sweet Jesus," he let out in a breath, watching her breasts tumble free.

Just like from a fantasy, Elandra reached up and pushed her hair back over her shoulders, making her breasts bounce with each swift movement. Kerith massaged her breasts, rubbing his thumbs over her sensitive nubs. He licked his lips and captured one breast in his mouth, suckling on it and enjoying the taste of her. She moaned in pleasure and ran her hands through his hair, pulling his head closer. He raked his teeth over her nub and gently nipped at her receptive skin. He brought his head up, eliciting a moan from her at the loss of his mouth against her. He gazed into her eyes, which had turned from their normal, gentle hazel to the darkest chestnut he had ever seen. He stood up from the bed and offered his hand. Elandra stared at it for a moment, confused, and felt her breath hitch as she felt the electricity and heat pouring off him. She took his hand and gently rose, following him down the hall, letting the sweatpants and her rose underwear fall to the floor as they went.

He brought her into the bedroom and motioned toward the bed. "Here."

She walked toward the bed, placed a hand on the sheets, and turned to him. "What, you can only do it in your own bed?" she asked, her voice coy and sultry at the same time.

Before he had time to answer, she walked up to him and leaned toward him, whispering into his ear, "That's okay, because I have so much I can do to you."

She gently ran her tongue around the outside of his ear and kissed him. She started to withdraw, but was stopped when his arm snaked around her waist. She gave him a seductive smile, knowing she was in control. He pulled her into a kiss, and as their tongues found their groove, she turned them around so his back was to the bed.

"Let me show you what real passion looks like!" She harshly pushed him back.

He allowed himself to fall onto the bed. She ran her eyes up his body and licked her lips as she stared into his eyes. She knelt down onto the bed and slowly started crawling up to him. He fought to keep his hands at his sides as he watched her make her way up to him like a hungry tigress. She rose up and met his eyes. His newfound erection strained beneath his pants and reached for pleasure between her thighs, and she bent down and claimed him with a heated kiss.

He broke the kiss and looked deep into her stunned eyes. "No, Elandra, let me show you how to feel."

He grabbed her hips and tossed her onto her back. He climbed on top, and in one fell swoop, he shed his jeans and boxers. He leaned across and pulled open the drawer of the nightstand, removing a condom. Her eyes were glued to his every movement, and she watched as he rolled it on. She licked her lips, drinking in the sight of him. She ran her finger up his body, directing his gaze to her face. He nestled himself in between her legs, poising himself at her slick entrance.

She reached up and nipped at his neck. "Mmm…I want you in me, Kerith."

He paused for a moment, looking up into her lust-filled eyes. "I want you to go with me."

"Anything you want." She cooed, and then added, "As long as you get in me now!"

He chuckled, loving her brashness, and then he gave her what she craved. He dove into the depths between her legs, and they both moaned in ecstasy. They moved together in pleasure, feeling it taking them higher and higher.

"Oh, god, Elandra," he panted.

"Are you ready?" she asked in between moans.

"For what?" he asked, panting.

"To let your body be consumed by the intense fire!" She grinned at him, grabbed his lower cheeks, and pulled him in hard as she thrust her hips up. "Oh, god! Yes, Kerith!"

Their screams and moans lasted for what seemed like hours as he let her ride out her orgasm, and he fought to remain in control as she clenched around him. As Elandra came down from her peak, she ran her hands up his back, and they both sighed with content. Kerith slowly started to pull out and then paused. Their eyes locked and darkened. Elandra wearily shook her head yes, and Kerith wrapped his arms around her back, grabbing her shoulders. He took a deep breath and kissed her gently. He then drove hard and fast, filling her completely and reaching nerves she never knew existed. She raked her nails down his back, he withdrew to the point of exit, and then, together, they drove so hard and fast that their screams of pleasure melted into one. They rode out their explosive orgasms together, and she clenched tightly around him as they shivered and shook together. Then they collapsed, still connected, into the softness of the bed. They panted and tried to collect themselves as they looked into each other's eyes. It was Kerith who moved first, lifting his weight from her and slowly withdrawing. Elandra gave a small sigh of loss as he rolled onto his back.

"Don't think you're staying that far away there, missy!" Kerith said as he grabbed her arm and rolled her on top of him.

They lay, stomach to stomach. Elandra's left leg arched at the knee, and her left arm draped over his body toward his shoulder as her head lay on his chest, facing her raised arm. He lay with his legs straight out, his right arm resting on her raised leg, and his left arm hugging her possessively around her waist. They fell gently asleep, beaded with sweat and a blanket covering nothing but their lower halves.

Chapter 9

He woke up to the smell of fresh-brewing coffee and rolled over to find his bed empty. He gently ran his hand over the sheets, and images of the night before went flashing through his head. His mind ran backward through the night: him kissing Elandra's shoulder; their entwined bodies; their frantic rush to get clothes off; the initial passion in their first kiss. His mind came to a screeching halt as he remembered why they had come to his apartment: the rain, her tears, her intense fear ,and the damaged body she had carried through the storm. He pounded his fist into the bed. *Someone had hurt Elandra!* Fear flooded his veins—she wasn't in bed with him. Where was she? He jumped out of bed, threw on a T-shirt and jeans, and ran out of the room.

He raced down the one hallway toward the kitchen. "Dammit Elandra! Please don't be stupid." He prayed, "Don't have been stupid and gone home."

At the end of the hall, he came to a screeching halt. His eyes scanned the kitchen, and all he saw was the freshly brewed coffee. He ran his eyes over the floor and found only his sweatpants.

He pounded his fist into the wall. "Dammit, Elandra!"

"What'd I do?"

Kerith whipped around to find Elandra perched in the corner of the couch, clutching a coffee mug in her hand with the paper spread out in front of her.

"Jesus Christ, woman." Kerith ran his hand through his hair.

"Again, what'd I do?" she asked, her voice calm as day.

Kerith rushed over, cupped her face in his hands, and kissed her with overwhelming protective passion.

"Well morning to you, too. But I still want to know what I did." She hugged her mug tight in her hands as she drained its contents.

"I'd thought you…" his voice trailed off as he spotted the newspaper. He pointed at it. "I don't get the paper." His voice started to rise in anger and panic. "Dammit, woman! I told you to stay here. Who knows what could have happened to you!" he shouted.

"Jeez, relax, Reid." Elandra rose from the couch and walked over to the coffee maker. She took a mug and started filling it with coffee. "I didn't go out." She handed Kerith the mug and returned to her perch on the couch, "I swiped it from someone else's doormat."

Kerith walked over and sat down beside her. "You mean you didn't go buy one?"

"No."

His shoulders relaxed, and he crumpled into the back of the couch. He ran a hand through his hair and let his head lull back on the cushions. Elandra reached over and took the mug from his hands, curling it in her hands and taking a sip.

A sly smile tugged at the corners of her mouth. "I mean all I did was go down the street and steal one from someone else's doorstep."

Kerith bolted upright, "You what? Dammit, Elandra! You took a beating last night. I brought you here 'cause you were all banged up. I go out of my way to keep you safe, and you go out on your own?"

Elandra's lips curved into a vicious smile, and she laughed, "Relax, Reid. I'm kidding. I stole the paper from your neighbor across the hall." She handed the coffee over to Reid and watched him take a sip, savoring the way his lips hugged the cup.

He ran a hand through his hair, a move Elandra had become accustomed to as being a reflex when he was stressed, "Dammit, woman, what are you trying to do? Give me a heart attack?" He rolled his neck.

"No, but it's nice to know you care." She chuckled, "You treat all your cases like this? Very hands-on approach?"

"You want hands-on, eh?" He rose, placed the cup on the table, took her hands and pulled her to her feet. "Well then, maybe…" He spun her around and placed her hands on the back of the couch, bending her over slightly. "I should frisk you."

He ran his hands up her arms and down to her waist. She could feel him quickly growing hard as he pressed his length into her. She leaned back into him, resting her head on his shoulder and taking in the scent she had come to establish as his own. She brought her left arm up and started to stroke his cheek, eliciting a cross between a moan and growl from him. He quickly spun her around to face him and pulled her into a deep and devouring kiss. She pressed her body closer to his, and they both enjoyed the way their bodies melded perfectly together. He started kissing down her neck, her hands roving over his back and pulling his shirt out from his pants. Her head lulled back as he continued his attack on her senses. She snaked her hands around and took hold of his belt. She freed it from its loop and was in the middle of pulling it free from his pants when the phone rang. He continued to suckle and nip at her body.

"Shouldn't you get that?" she asked, wishing they didn't have to end this.

"If it's important, they'd call my cell." He pressed a kiss to the top of her breast, suckling through her shirt. "They can call back."

She moaned as she fell into his drive, but was left nagging as the phone continued to ring.

He noticed that her attention was drifting. "Pay no attention to it," he commanded.

Elandra's body froze at his words. "Did you just give me an order?"

"Yes, now do what I said. Ignore it." He focused his attention back on her neck.

Elandra started to pull back just as his cell phone began to ring. "Answer it," she snapped, anger shooting through her veins.

"Ignore it. It can't be anything important, and besides, we're busy here," he replied, trying to pull her back into his embrace.

She held her arms out, warding him off. "Not anymore we're not. Answer it!" The fire he had started inside her turned to one of rage.

Kerith blew out a breath. "Fine! But I don't understand what your problem is."

Elandra crossed her arms over her chest. "Just answer it," she clipped.

Kerith walked over, picked up his cell phone, and started mumbling into it, keeping his voice low enough that Elandra couldn't hear what he was saying.

How could he? How could he give me an order? I'm not one of his officers or something. Elandra's thoughts raged on, *this man is impossible. Why the hell did I have sex with such a jackass? Because it was great sex, sex like nothing before, it had the passion you're trying to teach;* a little voice called to her in her head. *Oh, right. But the man is an ass.*

Kerith hung up the phone and looked at her. "Grab your coat, we're going."

Another order—Elandra couldn't believe it. Who the hell did he think he was? No one ordered her around like that!

His face was concealed in seriousness. "Come on, we have to go to the station." He sighed, seeing she wasn't moving. "It's about Chloe."

Chloe…right, he was investigating Chloe's death. She'd never follow his order, but she got her coat and followed him out the door. While in the car, Elandra rationalized with herself that she wasn't following orders, she was doing this for Chloe. The sooner they figured this out, the sooner she could get away from Reid, the asshole! She suddenly felt a pang of absence—with him went the passionate sex she herself had only dreamed about.

Kerith sat in the car, more focused on Elandra then on the road. He looked at her out of the corner of his eye; she had changed back into her skirt. It looked sexy, but somehow Elandra also made it look incredibly comfortable. He fought to keep his hands on the wheel, but was still confused as to her sudden iciness. *Why do women always do this? Why won't she just tell me what's wrong?* He let out a deep breath. He couldn't explain it, but Elandra's cold reaction to him hurt. But something in his head drove a message into his mind: *She can be cold all she wants, right now, but I've got to break through her barriers.* As Kerith pulled into a spot at the station, he decided that, no matter what, he would break through the walls that held Elandra back, and she would be his.

Chapter 10

The heavy door swung wide open. "Now you stay right with me and don't say anything. Believe me, a girl like you walking in and all hell will break loose," Kerith ordered in a low voice.

"A girl like me? What is that suppose to mean?" Elandra asked with a hint of indignation.

"I mean, just look at you."

"What, the skirt? So you're back on the idea that I'm running a whorehouse, are you? And you're saying I look like a hooker?" Her voice rose with each question.

"Shh, no, I'm just saying, when a gorgeous women like you walks in, the whole precinct takes notice, and basically all work freezes while every guy checks her out."

"Oh." Elandra's voice was barely above a whisper. "You think I'm gorgeous?" she fished, cracking a sly smile.

Kerith turned back and faced her. "Of course I do." He took her hand in his. "Now just keep your mouth shut, and we'll get out of here in one piece—"

He was cut off by a voice from behind him. "Well, Kerith, I thought you weren't supposed to bring your work home with you."

Kerith gritted his teeth and turned, holding Elandra's hand behind his back. "Reilly…"

"Damn, Kerith, if that's the kind of case you got, hell, I'll trade ya. I'm chasing car thieves, and I know they don't look anything like that," Reilly added with an appreciative laugh.

"That's enough, Riley," Kerith said through clenched teeth, taking a step away from Elandra and releasing her hand.

"Hey, Kerith, really. I mean, look at her." Reilly looked Elandra up and down. "Hey, guys, look what Reid brought in," he called to the room.

A group of cops slowly sauntered up to join them. Elandra blushed at the attention and smiled at Kerith, glancing at him out of the corner of her eye.

A whistle came up from the crowd as a man stepped forward. "Damn. Kerith, you are one lucky bastard. Hey, honey, if Reid doesn't meet your expectations, you come find me. The name's Alden, Luc Alden. And I can make your every wish come true." He grinned at her.

Elandra giggled, and Kerith grabbed her hand. "There's no worries there," he stated sharply. "She won't be needing you, Alden. We need to see the chief, so we'll be going now." He started to pull Elandra away.

"Well, Reid, I'm sure if Alden can't help her, then someone else can," Reilly stated, halting Kerith and Elandra in their tracks. "Believe me, miss, we have a very dedicated team, isn't that right boys?"

A resounding chorus of agreement dispersed throughout the room.

Kerith started once more pulling Elandra down the hall. "See, that's the kind of thing I was talking about. We're here not even five minutes, and you got guys lining up for you," he grumbled.

"Well if I didn't know any better Reid, I would say you're jealous," Elandra said with a slight giggle of triumph as she took quick steps in her duct-taped high heels, trying to keep up.

"Well, they're a bunch of animals. They show no respect to women," he muttered.

"Yeah, but is the mighty Detective Reid actually jealous?" Elandra played. "Reid?" She felt her heart flutter with excitement at the thought of driving a man to jealousy.

Kerith was saved from answering her question as he reached for the doorknob and was met by an opening door.

"Thank you, Senator Prescott, you've been a great help," came a voice from inside the office.

Kerith stepped back as the figure in the door tipped his hat and started out. Elandra's breath hitched, and she gasped. She quickly skittered behind Kerith and gripped the back of his jacket. She felt her fear from the night before come flooding back.

"What? What are you doing?" he asked quizzically.

"That's him," she whispered. "That's the guy that attacked me last night."

"No problem, Chief Phillip. I felt it only right to come in, I knew you would get to me at some point, and I felt it best to be up front and let you know what happened."

He stepped out, facing Kerith and Elandra. "Detective. Ma'am." He tipped his hat to Elandra and walked off.

Elandra stared after him as Kerith turned to face her, holding her arms in his hands. "Are you sure that was him?"

Words couldn't get past Elandra's lips, so she nodded her consent. Kerith moved his left hand up to cup her face and stroke her cheek with his thumb.

"Shh, it's all right, sugar. I promise you I'm not gonna let him near you." He wiped a lone tear away, "You got me?" He guided her head up to meet his gaze.

She nodded once more. "Okay."

"Sugar? That you, Reid? Get your ass in here! I got some news you're gonna wanna hear."

"I'm not letting him near you, I promise." Kerith kissed her forehead.

"Reid!" the voice bellowed once more.

"Coming, sir." Kerith took Elandra's hand and led her into the office before them.

"Now, Reid, that was Senator Prescott. He just let me in on some info concerning the night of that Pattel girl's death," the chief stated without looking up from his desk, "Now he says—" He looked up and stumbled over his words upon seeing Elandra. "Oh. You brought company. How may we help you, miss?"

"This is Miss Rosedale, Chief. She owns Hidden Desires."

"You mean the place that hooker worked?" the chief asked in confusion.

"I can assure you, we are not a whorehouse, as is the common belief around here," Elandra stated in a clipped tone.

The chief looked at her with hooded eyes. "Look, miss, we're not looking to bust up your little pleasure palace. Right now we just want to figure out who murdered the girl. So don't get your panties in a twist."

"Pleasure palace? I'll have you know—" Elandra started, but was waved off by Kerith.

"Shh, sugar. Let me handle this," he soothed, his irritation rising at the chief's suspicions.

"Sugar? What, are you sleeping with her, Reid?" the chief snorted.

Elandra blushed and looked away, while Kerith stood there in stunned silence.

"That's what I thought. Dammit, Kerith, you don't sleep with suspects," the chief muttered angrily.

"Suspect?" the words barely passed Elandra's lips.

"She's runs a goddamn whorehouse! We worked things out with Sass so we could control this type of thing. And now you're sleeping with the woman who is trying to upset our system. Goddammit, Kerith! I expected more sense out of you. A goddamn whorehouse!" he started shouting.

Elandra felt anger starting to boil in her veins. She was a suspect. *So that's why he slept with me, to try to get me to admit to Chloe's murder. And to add insult to injury they still think I run a whorehouse!*

"Listen here, I have a degree in psychology, I graduated top of my class, and I run a very reputable business! I do not run a goddamn whorehouse! My girls are not prostitutes!" Elandra started to yell back.

"Well then, some of the girls are doing extra work behind your back!" the chief yelled back, standing up.

"Not a chance. The girls know I would never stand for it. It's the one rule I am adamant about. My girls are not allowed to become involved with our clients, relationship-wise, or even simply for sex," Elandra explained in a sharp tone, unable to hide the hurt from the accusation.

"Well then, someone has no regard for your rules. Senator Prescott came here to inform me that he was with Ms. Pattel the night she was killed." He sat back down and looked at Kerith. "Did you tell her where we found the body?"

"Yes, sir." Kerith directed his gaze to the floor.

"Well let me explain again, Miss Rosedale. Ms. Pattel's body was found at the motel just off the highway. She met Senator Prescott there; he admits that he hired her that night."

"Hired her?" Elandra asked in shock, feeling her heart break.

"Hired her for sex. He says he got her name from one of your employees, and seeing as she was also one of your employees…well, you can see where we get the idea you run a prostitution ring," he said without care.

Elandra stood there in shock, took a deep breath, and conceded, "All right, I admit that he was a client of ours—" Elandra was cut off.

"Client? So you admit you hire prostitutes," the chief blurted out sharply.

Elandra took a deep breath, trying to center herself. "His girlfriend came to us, asking for our help. It's unusual to get someone like him as a client, but I agreed. We teach men how to demonstrate passion and what kind of attention some women crave."

"Fine, you had no clue it was going on, but that still doesn't prove that it wasn't happening."

Elandra felt crushed. Her girls...her girls... prostitutes...being paid for sex...sex...Elandra's head jerked up at the memory. "Chief, it may be that some of my girls are working on the side, however..." she drifted off, leaning forward and placing both hands on the desk.

"However? You have a theory? Well then, miss, by all means, do share it." He placed his hands behind his head, leaned back, and placed his feet up on his desk.

"Last night I was attacked," Elandra proudly stated, standing straight up.

The chief paused, waiting for more, but nothing more was said. "That's it? You were attacked? Believe me, Miss Rosedale, I'm sorry you were attacked, and we'll look into it, but I'm not sure I see how that connects with the Pattel girl's death."

"Because it was the senator that attacked me!" Elandra stated triumphantly. "He attacked me, and his admitting to being with Chloe that night gives him the opportunity."

"Senator Prescott attacked you?" the chief asked in disbelief.

"Yes, and it's not the first time, either."

"What?" Kerith muttered, touching Elandra's left arm, "I thought it was the mob making a move 'cause you wouldn't work with them."

"What? Victor Prescott is a well-respected senator!" the chief bellowed, his feet hitting the floor. He now completely ignored Kerith.

"I don't care if he's the president! He attacked me last night!" Elandra yelled.

The chief took a deep breath. "Look, do you understand the implications?"

"I understand that he attacked me," she replied, crossing her arms before her chest.

"Listen, it was dark, right? You probably couldn't tell what he looked like. It could have been anybody," he continued in a calm tone, he raising a hand to halt Elandra's objections. "Besides, Senator Prescott was at a charity function last night."

"Or so he says."

"Elandra has a point, chief. It's not unusual for politicians to lie." Kerith added, causing Elandra to turn and stare at him in shock.

"Well, he's not lying."

"How do you know?" She glared back at the chief, tears pricking at her eyes.

"Because he was at the same benefit for the children's hospital that I was at. That's how I know."

*

With all the commotion going on in the office, no one noticed the man who had been standing outside, listening, walk quietly away and out of the station.

*

She stretched out on the bed, reaching her hands high above her head. She rolled over onto her back and reached to the bedside table. She pulled the package down to her. *Now time to work,* she thought. She nimbly drew a single cigarette from its home, placed the pack down on the table, and took up the lighter. She lit the cigarette and drew a few deep breaths from it. She looked over at the man lying beside her and felt an all-too-familiar pain form between her eyes.

"Tell me a story, Zach." Her voice was sweet as sugar.

"Honey, you know I'm no good at it." He looked over at her and yawned.

"Aw, pretty please…" She rolled over onto her stomach. "Come on. You're a city councilor, Mr. Zachary Brenner." She giggled, "You're a politician. Of course you can tell stories."

Zach looked over at her. "Sorry, sweetie, I can't tell stories," he chuckled.

She sighed dramatically. "Well, then tell me a story about work. Come on, I might as well get my money's worth, I know you do. Or at least I hope you do." She put on an innocent, concerned tone.

He smiled at her. "Oh, no, baby. You're worth every penny I pay you."

She giggled, "See? What do you need a secretary for, when you got me?"

He stroked her bare back. "That is true. My wife would suspect something if I slept with my secretary." He pulled her over to him. "But I keep you, my own private hooker, and Shelly's none the wiser." He chuckled, "Now…" He leaned forward and kissed the top of her head. "Let me tell you a story about work." He shifted her so her head rested on his chest. "You'll like this one. The mayor has a secret love for indecent pictures of little boys…"

Chapter 11

Eandra stormed out of the chief's office, and the officers parted like the Red Sea as she thundered through the station. She pushed the doors open with an echoing bang as she poured into the street. Every eye in the station followed her out and then looked pityingly as Kerith raced past.

"God, I'm glad I'm not him right now," Reilly said to Kerith's passing back.

"Hell hath no fury like a woman scorned," Luc added, chuckling.

Reilly looked over at him. "Then that must have been one hell of a meeting with the chief."

"Remind me never to introduce a girl I'm sleeping with to the chief." Luc let out a laugh deep from in his belly.

"You won't need to worry about that if you don't get back to work, Alden, 'cause I'll bury you so deep in paperwork you'll never get to sleep with another woman," Chief Phillip bellowed as he surveyed the room. He turned and started heading back to his office. "Jesus Christ, Reid.

What have you gotten yourself into now?" he muttered under his breath.

*

Kerith had to jog to catch up to Elandra, and once he did, he had to grab her arm to get her attention.

"Hey, where's the fire?"

Elandra turned and ripped her arm from his grip. "Don't touch me, Reid!"

Kerith held his hands up in surrender. "Whoa, there. Where's the fire and brimstone coming from?"

Elandra glared at him. "Where did it come from? You're the *detective*, you tell me."

"Okay, hold on." He took a step back. "White flag, here; I surrender. I don't know what I did, but I'd sure love to make up for it."

Elandra placed one hand on her hip and brought the other up to give her a pensive look, "Hmm…could it maybe have to do with everyone still thinking I run a whorehouse? Or maybe that I'm apparently upsetting your precious system?" Kerith groaned, running a hand over his face, but Elandra just continued talking. "Or, wait a minute, what about this one?"

He looked up at her, afraid of her next words.

"Maybe it has to do with you sleeping with me because I'm a suspect, and you're trying to get me to confess to Chloe's murder!" she huffed. "Which I did not do, by the way," she added pointedly.

"I said I surrender," Kerith stated.

"Tell me, Detective Reid, do you sleep with every suspect in a hope that they'll confess to anything after they'd had the worst sex in their life?" Elandra felt her blood boiling over.

Kerith's hands dropped to his sides, "All right, that was a low blow, even for you." His tone turned sour.

"Even for me?" Elandra hissed, "Oh, please, Reid, do tell me what you think of me. Don't hold back on my account."

"Goddammit, woman!" he shouted. "You want to know what I think of you right now?"

Elandra crossed her arms and gave him a death glare. "Please."

"Right now I think you're a stubborn, self-righteous, and impossible-to-deal-with woman."

"Well...Well, I think you're a self-absorbed, manipulative jackass!" she shouted at him.

"I wasn't finished," he pointed out harshly.

Elandra was only able to utter a surprised, "Oh."

"You're also smart as hell, sexier than should be legal, dangerous as original sin, and massively turning me on right now." He snuffed, "But the police parking lot is no place to discuss this." His eyes glazed over in darkness as he looked at her.

Elandra's breath hitched as she realized what he said, and she looked around, reminding herself of where they were. Elandra blushed when she realized she was having a screaming match with a cop in front of his territory. "We need a less public place to finish this discussion," she stated meekly.

"Oh, just say it's an argument, for Pete's sake."

"All right, let's take this argument somewhere else," Elandra hammered out. "Someplace where we can be on even ground."

"Right, let's take this to my place." Kerith grabbed her hand and started heading to the car.

"Your place?"

"You got a better idea?" Kerith muttered through pursed lips.

"No, I guess not." Elandra sighed.

"Then let's get a move on, because I want to fuck you so bad right now."

*

Kerith threw the door open with furious force and dragged Elandra in behind him. He slammed the door, locked it, and turned back to Elandra.

"All right, let's finish that argument now." He moved forward as if to kiss her, but she placed a hand between them and stepped back.

"No, Reid, I need answers, and we will finish this argument."

Kerith ran a hand through his hair and let out a frustrated sigh, "Fine." He held his hand up directing them to the living room. "After you then, I'd rather we were farther from the sharp objects as you rip into me."

Elandra let out a frustrated growl, "Is that what you think of me?"

"Get serious, Elandra, of course not. I was trying to make a joke." He paused, looking at her imploringly. "You know, try to lighten the mood."

"Well, don't." She sat down on the couch with a huff.

"Fine." He threw his hands up in frustration.

They sat in silence for a few moments, Elandra stewing in her own thoughts and Reid trying to calm down his overexcited cock.

Elandra finally looked up at him; the mask of anger was gone and replaced with one of hurt. "Did you sleep with me just 'cause I'm a suspect?"

Kerith was taken back by the question. "Of course not."

"So you don't think I killed Chloe?"

"Definitely not. Someone who commits murder does not get attacked shortly after meeting with the police."

"Not even if someone is trying to make themselves look like an innocent victim?" she asked earnestly.

"Well, now you're starting to think like a cop." He smiled at her. "But I don't think you set up that attack on yourself last night. I know real victims when I see them, and no offense, but you were it."

"Thanks." Elandra smiled up at him and blushed.

"And anyway…" He pulled her over onto his lap. "…I slept with you because you are sexy as hell and full of fire. The fact that you were a suspect and it let me keep an eye on you was just a bonus."

Elandra's head jerked around to face him, "Keep an eye on me?"

"Ah, shit!" Kerith swore. "I screwed up, didn't I?"

Elandra leapt up off his lap. "You felt you needed to keep an eye on me?" She glared at him once more.

Kerith raised his hands up in his now-familiar surrender position, "Ah, shit, Elandra. I didn't mean it like that, sugar. I was trying to joke again. We were doing so well. Too soon?"

"A joke? That was supposed to be a joke? What kind of messed-up humor do you have?" Elandra felt as if steam were rolling off her in her anger.

"Apparently a poorly timed one." Kerith shrugged.

"Oh great! More jokes!" Elandra threw her hands up and made a growl in frustration.

"Ok, I get it." He ran a hand through his hair, "Not the time for jokes."

"No, it's not." Elandra walked past his bookcase wall into his makeshift office and stood by his desk.

Kerith walked in after her, "Okay, I'm sorry, Elandra," he sighed. "You being a suspect…" He raised his hand to stop her from interrupting. "…at the time, had nothing to do with me sleeping with you." He walked toward her with his arms outstretched. "I don't need a case, really anything at all, to make me want to sleep with you." He hugged his arms around her waist, pulling her back flush against him.

Elandra could feel his erect cock straining against his pants.

"See?" He kissed her neck. "All I need is you, and I'm ready." He kissed her ear and lightly bit it, causing Elandra to gasp.

"I'd do everything in my power to get thrown into jail if this were the punishment." Elandra tilted her head into his movements, and a small moan escaped from her lips. Kerith continued to kiss up and down her neck, sending tingling chills down her spine.

"Still think I slept with you 'cause you were a suspect?" he mumbled into her ear before nipping it again.

Elandra sighed her response, "No."

"Good." He turned her around to face him and backed her up against the desk. "'Cause I want your trust," he said in all honesty. "And besides, you're incredibly sexy when you're angry." His hands started to roam over her body as he continued to ravage her neck. "God I was ready to devour you, right there in the parking lot." Kerith's hand came up and cupped her breast as both their breaths became more labored. "While you look unbelievably sexy, and I love that skirt, it has to come off. Now!" he growled.

Kerith's movements were swift as he stripped her of her shirt and skirt. They came together for a deep embrace as Kerith fondled her breasts.

"Dear god, I love your breasts," he stated in between pants of breath, causing Elandra to giggle. He kissed her neck. "And I love the way you taste and feel." He crushed her with a kiss, and Elandra felt her knees go weak, but Kerith's strong arms held her upright. "Jesus Christ, I have to have you." He reached behind her and swiped at the desk, causing everything to fall crashing to the floor.

Elandra slid her panties down to her ankles and started to undo his belt. She looked up into his eyes. "You...you have my trust."

Kerith cupped her lower cheeks and lifted her onto the desk, all the time kissing her. He kissed her neck, her jaw, and the top of her breast. Elandra panted furiously as she pushed his pants down, revealing that he had decided to wear no boxers. Elandra silently thanked every denomination she could think of at that moment, and when she looked back down, she realized Kerith had slipped on a condom without her noticing.

"God, I want you," Elandra heard herself growl.

Kerith positioned himself at her opening and looked up into her eyes. "Yeah?"

"Yeah."

"How much? How much do you want me in you?" he teased, pushing in slightly. Elandra closed her eyes and moaned. She then sighed at the loss when he pulled back out. "How much?"

"God, more than anything."

"Look at me, Elandra. I want you to look at me when I enter you."

Elandra wiggled forward slightly, causing him to enter her slightly, and eliciting a moan from Kerith. She opened her eyes. "Get in me, Reid. Now!"

Kerith pulled out and positioned himself again. "Now that sounded like an order," he chuckled and looked up into her glaring eyes, dark with passion.

"It was. Now do it!" Elandra ordered.

"Jesus Christ, Elandra. It's fucking hot when you take control." He blew out a harsh breath. "I swear I just got harder; that's so fucking fabulous."

"Then do it!" Elandra continued, biting her lower lip and reveling in her power.

Kerith gently slid into her, eliciting a moan from both of them. He found a gentle rhythm and rocked them back and forth. Elandra's head lulled back in ecstasy, and Kerith's eyes screwed shut in pleasure. The room filled with their moans and sighs with every movement, and Elandra started to dig her fingers into Kerith's shoulders as they drove on. Without words, they both opened their eyes, and their gazes met.

Kerith drove into her with one more deep thrust that had them both coming apart at the seams. Kerith growled, and Elandra screamed her appreciation. They collapsed into each other; Elandra felt her whole body was drained.

Kerith was the first to stir. "I need a nap."

"Me, too," Elandra purred, wrapping her arms around him.

"Come on then, let's go." Elandra expected Kerith to pull out, but he shifted his hands under her and lifted her up with him still inside her.

Elandra giggled, "What are you doing?"

"I'm not leaving you, believe me," he groaned, "so I'm carrying you off to bed." He kicked off his pants and started making his way down the hall.

Elandra giggled again, "Okay, He-man."

Kerith made it to the bedroom and swung the door shut behind them. "Don't want people staring in," he laughed. Kerith sat them down on the bed. "Not that they wouldn't have had a show at the window there."

Elandra blushed crimson red, and she made to remove herself from him.

"Just where do you think you're going, young lady?" He held her tightly in place.

"I'm cold." She stuck out her tongue. "So I'm going to put on one of your sweatshirts." She hopped off his lap.

Kerith moaned at the loss, "But I don't want you to cover up." He pouted.

"Don't worry," she said as she opened his closet. "I'm taking off my bra first." She giggled as she disappeared behind the door.

"Dear god, if I could go again that quick." He laughed and fell back on the bed.

Elandra snaked her way back toward the bed and Kerith. She snuggled up next to him, and he threw the used condom in the bedside trash and placed an arm around her. Elandra curled into his body, and within moments, they were both fast asleep.

Chapter 12

The whole room seemed to shake as the door was slammed shut. His heavy footsteps echoed throughout the room as he walked toward the figure at the table. His prey didn't even flinch as he drew nearer, so he made no attempt to silence his pace. He walked up behind the figure and placed his hand on its shoulder. He waited until the figure turned to face him, and then…

SLAP!

He slapped the occupant across the face, and the sound echoed throughout the room.

"Jacob, you idiot!" he bellowed at the man in the chair. "Do you realize what you've done? Do you realize the danger you put us in? Put *me* in?"

The man sitting in the chair simply sat there silently and allowed his attacker to continue.

"You self-absorbed, little…" his voice trailed off as his anger took over. He stormed around the room. "How could you be so stupid? How could you risk everything we've worked for? All our plans? Do you realize the position you put us in? She recognized you! She pointed me out to the cops! How could you do this to me?" he raked a hand through his hair. "All you had to do was wait. But no, you had to go and risk it all! And for what? Some…for a…" He drew in a deep breath. "You risked everything for some dirty, insignificant little whore!"

"She's not a whore," came the quiet man's voice from the table.

He quickly turned and stared at the man. "What did you say?" his voice came, harsh but quiet.

"I said she's not a whore," the reply came, little more than a whisper.

"Jacob, you're an idiot. Of course she's a whore. She runs a whorehouse, you know that." He chuckled to himself, "She's a dirty little whore. She's probably serviced hundreds of men. Probably more travelled than all of America."

Jacob stood abruptly, throwing his chair back and letting it crash to the floor in the process. "Cassidy is not a whore!" he bellowed.

"Well, well, isn't this rich? You seem to be quite taken with her—first-name basis even." He continued laughing. "Taken in by a whore—"

Jacob charged at him, pushing the man's back up against a wall. "Don't call her that again!" he threatened.

The man took hold of Jacob's arms and threw them down. "How dare you!" He pushed away from the wall, "How dare you threaten me! I'm the one who's protected you, looked out for you. How dare you do this!" he yelled as he stalked toward Jacob. "I took you in and looked after you when no one else would! You owe your life to me!" He raised his arm as if to hit Jacob. "I'm in control; I'm the one who calls the shots. I decide who and when!" He took a deep breath and lowered his arm. "I decide."

He walked up to Jacob and placed his hand on his cheek. "I'm just looking out for you, Jacob. I always will. But…but she's…she's dangerous. Do you see that?" He angled his head trying to look into Jacob's downcast eyes. "Do you understand? She's a threat, and you have to stay away from her." He guided Jacob's face up and looked straight in his eyes. "She's trouble, Jacob. You have to listen to me. I'm just trying to protect you, like I always have." He pulled Jacob into a hug. "You have to stay away from her." He pulled back and held Jacob's face in both hands. "Do you understand me? You have to stay away from her. Are you listening to me, Jacob? You need to stay away from that whore." He paused, waiting for Jacob to nod his head yes. "For your own good, stay away from her."

He turned and quietly walked out of the room, leaving Jacob standing there. Jacob's voice, barely above a whisper, echoed throughout the room, "Cassidy is not a whore. She belongs to me."

✳

The door opened without a sound, "Anything interesting or should I have brought a book?" Kerith asked.

Luc turned around on the metal chair. "Same as always. She's been a busy girl today—a city councilor and a CEO. And if the tap's right, then she's got a congressman tonight." He stood up and stretched. "Where this girl gets her energy is beyond me. If I wasn't such a great cop, I might go after her myself."

Kerith snorted in disbelief. "You're mediocre at best, Alden. Don't leave me for dreams of grandeur." He walked forward and handed Luc a cup of coffee. "Thought you could use this."

Luc laughed, "Are you kidding me? After watching her going at it, I'm ready and rearing to go. Hell, it's lucky I'm getting off in time to head to the bars and find a friend for the night." He took the coffee anyway. "Good luck, you're going to need it," he tossed over his shoulder as he walked out of the room.

Kerith took his place on the metal chair facing the window and settled in for a long watch. He picked up the binoculars from the windowsill. "So let's see what Miss Mercedes is doing today." As usual, Mercedes was getting undressed, but for an unusual twist, she was by herself.

Kerith leaned back in the chair and put his heels up on the windowsill. Kerith let his mind wander through the events of the past couple of days. He closed his eyes, and immediately, images of Elandra floated through his brain—her smooth skin, soft hair, long legs, and the way she arched into him when they made love. Kerith heaved a delighted sigh as he played through some of her simple movements, running her hand through her hair, her placing her hand on his hips, and the way she dug her nails into his back. Kerith let out a chuckle. *Oh, man, am I in trouble. I haven't felt this way about a woman since Stephanie; hell I don't think I even felt like this with her. And Elandra's hell, too. I've never met a more independent, stubborn, pig-headed, and frustrating woman. But I also won't find another more strong-willed, smart, attractive, and beyond sexy woman in my lifetime.*

Kerith opened his eyes with a smile on his face, dropped his feet to the ground, and ran a hand through his hair. *Good god, this woman is getting me twisted in knots. Come on, man, focus on the job.* He cleared his throat and picked up the binoculars again. "Shit," he muttered under his breath, "she's at it again." He put the binoculars down and picked up a camera. He zoomed in on the couple. "She just never stops." He started snapping pictures and paused after five. He lowered the camera and rolled his neck. "Sex, it's always about sex." He ran a hand through his hair, trying to fend off his growing frustration. He pulled the camera back up and zoomed in again to watch as Mercedes bounced up and down on her newest guest. He focused on the sweat now glistening her body, and watched as her mouth fell open in ecstasy.

He closed his eyes to try to keep his growing erection at bay, but was only met with images of Elandra withering below him in the throes of an orgasm. He screwed his eyes tighter, but it only sharpened the images in his mind. He gave a frustrated groan as his hand went to the zipper on his pants. He slowly slid down the small piece of metal, as his mind continued to assault him with images of Elandra as he drove into her. He freed his eager cock, and it grew further under his touch. He slowly started to stroke himself as his memory started to whisper her moans and sighs. His hand continued to slowly slide along his shaft as he pretended it was Elandra's slick, moist body enveloping him. Kerith screwed his eyes tightly shut as his movements grew more driven and eager.

A loud *thunk* echoed through the room, causing Kerith to jump from the seat. He looked beside the chair and realized he had dropped the camera. "Shit." He ran a nervous hand through his hair and looked up out the window. He was mesmerized with the continuing porn film that was playing itself out across the way. Kerith felt a slight breeze coming from the window and suddenly realized that his pants were still around his knees and that his cock stood proud for all to see. "Aw, Christ." He quickly put himself back in order and zipped up his pants. He thumped back down onto the chair, ran a frustrated hand through his hair, and picked up the camera once more, focusing on the room he was supposed to be watching. He watched for a minute as the occupants continued to moan and groan in ecstasy. "Can't you even pause for a break?" He closed his eyes to it once more and was again met with images of Elandra. "This woman will be the death of me," he groaned. He opened his eyes and focused on the task at hand; he lifted the camera and started snapping shots, "This is going to be one hell of a long night."

Chapter 13

Elandra shut off the water from the shower, stepped out, and cocooned herself in a towel. She looked in the mirror, her eyes quickly being drawn to her scar. She stared at the reflection of the rough *H*, its strong but smooth strokes staring back at her. It had taken some research, but she had figured out what the pattern was; it was *chikara*, the Kanji symbol for power. The image haunted her dreams some nights and had altered her days from the moment it touched her skin. Dark images of that fateful night flashed into her mind, her nose filled with the remembered smell of lavender— she still couldn't stand to have lavender near her. Heavy pants echoed in her ears, fear crept through her veins, and a chill ran over her skin. The images continued to flash before Elandra's eyes, images of the man above, moving slowly, savoring each moment; of the full moon and the trees surrounding her; a branded ring on a chain dangling in her face and the brand coming down on her chest. Her own scream pierced her ears, and she jolted back to reality.

Elandra shook herself free of the past and walked out into her bedroom. She approached her closet and drew the doors back, glancing at her wardrobe. She ran her hand across her choices: black, red, flannel, lace...her hand finally rested on her cerulean silk negligee with the black lace accents. She slipped into it with perfect ease, took a seat in front of her pink and white Victorian vanity, and tied her hair up with a slick, green ribbon. She moved with the grace of a ballerina over to the bed, gently drew back the covers, and slid in. She reached over to her nightstand and picked up a file, spreading it on her lap.

"Let's see here," she muttered to herself, flipping through the pages, "Stanley; well, first off, with a name like that, it's no wonder you've come to us. Hmm...his profile says he's a visual learner. Okay, he's mild mannered and shy. He needs someone who's brash in order to draw him out of his shell. Sounds like Mercedes to me—she can play her New York café waitress again." She giggled as she made notes on the paper. "Okay, who's next? Ramón; hmm...name like that, why are you here? Oh, CEO wife—of course. Okay, you need hands-on learning. Hmm...thinks he knows everything, but not gentle. That is definitely a cowgirl Chloe thing..." She started to write and paused, her hand hovering over the paper. "Chloe... that's right. Oh, my darling girl, what happened to you?" A tear slowly slid down her cheek. "Oh, Chloe..." She sniffed and wiped at her eyes. "Okay, I'm not going to get anything done if I'm crying." She sighed and closed the file. "All right..." She shook all the pain away.

She laid the file back on her bedside table and quickly turned off the light. She settled into her covers, and with a deep sigh, closed her eyes for sleep.

*

The wood frame of the window slid along his fingers effortlessly as he glided through the night with the stealth and grace of a cat. He straddled the branch without difficulty and slid the sill up without a sound. He reached across and pulled himself into the room; he softly rolled onto the floor and fought not to disturb the room's inhabitant. He glided over to the bed and crouched beside it, letting his eyes devour the image before him. His gaze slowly traced the outline in the bed, and he reached up and smoothed a strand of hair away from her face.

"You still feel the same, Cassidy." His feather-light touch and hushed tone didn't even stir her.

He sat back and silently watched her sleep through the night. By sunrise, he knew it was no longer safe to stay by her side.

He stood and placed a soft kiss on her forehead, "You are mine, Cassidy. Mine and mine alone." He stood back up and admired her still form. "I found you again, and this time I'm not letting you go. You belong to me, my little firecracker."

And he slipped out of the room just as quietly as he had slipped in, closing the window gently behind him.

*

Elandra woke with the morning sun warming her skin. She stretched and welcomed the refreshed and relaxed feeling that had overcome her entire body. Elandra turned toward the window to soak in the sun and froze in terror. On the white satin pillow placed beside her, Elandra spied the contrast of a sprig of lavender wrapped in a red ribbon. She shook with fear as she reached across and picked it up. Her hand shook as the reality hit her: someone had been in her room; someone had been there while she slept. Her mind reeled as she ran through the ideas. *Someone was here…lavender means devotion…while I slept…red means passion…someone was here…*

A harsh gasp escaped her lips as she examined the lavender and dropped it to the floor with a scream, for as she turned it, she felt cool metal contact with her skin. It landed with a thud, and Elandra threw back the covers, jumping from the bed. She hesitantly walked and picked up the lavender, examining it closer. She ran her hand over the ring attached by the ribbon and felt her skin crawl.

"No, it couldn't be…" her voice came barely above a whisper.

She traced her fingers along its raised edges, and the familiar, yet horrifying, symbol they formed. She placed her other hand on her skin and ran it down her collarbone to her scar. She stared down at the ring that had branded her all those years ago.

Elandra's whole body shook as she walked across the room to her telephone. "He can't be here. He can't know I'm here…" Her voice trailed off as she dialed. "Oh, please be there, please…" Elandra held her breath as the phone continued to ring. "It really was him the other night."

Images of the night she was attacked outside the Red Dragon swirled around in her mind, mixing with images from the night she was originally attacked and branded. Elandra's mind raced so fast in a sea of fear and confusion that she almost didn't hear the voice on the other end of the phone.

"Hello? Is anyone there? This is Detective Reid. Hello?"

Chapter 14

Kerith looked through the shop window, searching for Elandra. She'd seemed agitated and terrified when he had talked to her on the phone. As his eyes travelled the room, he found her. Kerith watched as Elandra sat and played with a package of sugar. He watched as her hands jittered, holding the sugar and nervously placing it back in its holder. He laughed as she started to place the packages in order, grouping them by kind. He walked into the shop, sending the bell over the door jingling merrily along. Kerith walked silently up behind her and noticed her hunched shoulders and tense stance. He moved and sat across from her, touching her shoulder as he went.

Elandra started at his touch and gave a sigh of relief. "Reid." She started to rise.

"No, sit. Please." Kerith motioned for her to resume her seat. "I want to know what happened. I want to know—"

He was cut off by the approach of the waiter.

"What can I get for you, sir?" the waiter asked.

"Just a coffee, thanks." Kerith's eyes never left Elandra's downcast face.

"Um, what kind of coffee?"

"What?" Kerith asked, finally looking up, an eyebrow rising in question.

"What kind of coffee, sir? We have lattes, cappuccinos, decafs, roasts, blends…"

"I just want coffee."

"Yes sir, but we have over twenty-five kinds of coffee." The waiter asked, a little exasperated.

"Do you have regular coffee? You know black, one flavor, the real kind? None of that fancy fruity stuff?"

"We have fifteen different fruit-flavored coffees, sir."

Elandra muffled a laugh behind her hand, finally looking up at Kerith.

"Oh, you think this is funny, do you?" Kerith asked her, smiling and teasing.

"How about you bring him a hazelnut whip, Peter," Elandra stated, her gaze never leaving Kerith's.

The waiter walked away in a frustrated silence.

"So, what's going on?" Kerith asked. "You sounded agitated on the phone."

"Someone broke into the house last night," Elandra stated, averting her gaze.

"What? Were you hurt? How did he get in?" Kerith's voice burst throughout the room.

Elandra leaned across the table and placed a hand over his to help calm him. "No one was hurt. Everything is fine. Nothing was taken, but something was left," her words tumbled out.

"You're okay." Kerith breathed a sigh of relief. "Wait. Did you say nothing was taken, but something was left?"

"Yes." Elandra drew a deep breath. "If you are to truly understand, then I have to tell you the whole story."

They paused as the waiter returned and gave Kerith his coffee. "What the hell is this?"

Elandra laughed, "It's called a 'hazelnut whip,' Reid."

"What's all this white stuff on top?" he asked in confusion.

"It's called whip cream. It really is good." She reached her hand across and scooped a bunch of the white cream onto her finger and placed it in her mouth. "Try it." She smiled.

Kerith moaned and took a small sip. "Mmm...all right, I give. It's good." He smiled back at her. "So tell me what's going on, Elandra."

Elandra's face fell, and she reached into her purse and pulled out the sprig of lavender.

"They left you lavender?" Kerith asked in total confusion. "Well, that's not really bad."

"I'm going to tell you something that I've never told a living soul." Elandra drew in another deep breath, trying to calm her nerves. She reached into her purse once more and drew out the brand, placing on the table in front of Kerith.

Kerith picked it up. "It's just a ring," he said, turning it over in his hands and taking a closer look at it. "Wait a minute. This looks familiar. This symbol..."

"It's not just a ring, it's a brand," Elandra whispered.

"It looks just like your scar—" Kerith's gaze rose from the ring, and he took in Elandra's downcast eyes and defeated look.

"It's what made my scar," Elandra conceded.

Kerith reached his hand out and lifted her chin, raising her eyes to meet his. "Tell me what happened, sugar."

Elandra's eyes started to glisten with unshed tears. "When I was nineteen, I always cut through the park on my way home from work; it had always been safe. But one night it became my worst nightmare." Elandra paused, terrified as the memory flowed through her mind.

Kerith held her hand on hers and folded his fingers around hers. "It's all right, you can tell me."

"That night I was attacked." Elandra drew a breath for strength. "I was raped that night…"

Kerith moved his chair so he sat beside her, and he stroked her cheek, "Oh, honey…"

"He tied my hands above my head to a tree and my legs to two other trees. And he made me tell him my name and everything about me. He wanted to get to know me, and he…I fought him as hard as I could, but he…he was stronger than me…he…he did…he did so many horrible things to me," Elandra sniffed as the tears started to slide down her cheeks.

Kerith hugged her close to him as she cried into his shoulder. "Oh, Elandra…I'm so sorry."

Elandra sniffed and looked up at him. "He did so many horrible things to me, and when he was done, he branded me with that…that ring. And he made me swear never to tell a soul, otherwise he would go after my family. He said that I belonged to him, and if I ever told anyone, he would kill them. I couldn't let him do it. I couldn't let him hurt them."

"So you didn't tell anyone?"

"No, and it got easier to keep my family safe once my mom died. I went off to school and was able to keep my distance from them. I was able to change my name to protect them, and so he couldn't follow me. You see, he had looked me up after that night, and he sent things to my house; he'd sent me letters and things. I needed to change so he wouldn't follow me. So I changed everything, I left Cassidy Montgomery behind and became Elandra Rosedale. I finished school, then came here and started Hidden Desires. I thought I had left those ghosts behind me, but they're back. He's back."

"But how do you know it's him?"

"He was the one who attacked me the other night; when you found me. It was him—he told me himself."

"But how do you know it was him who broke into the house?"

"The park where he raped me...where he held me... was...it was filled with lavender. To this day I can't stand it. And that is the exact ring which he branded me with. He watched me sleep, Reid. I know he did..." Her voice trailed off in desperate fear, and her gaze fell.

"Oh, El, I'm so sorry I wasn't there to help." He rested his hand on her arm.

"It's all right, there's nothing you could have done." Her voice was filled with defeat, and her eyes remained glued to the table.

"I'll get an undercover uniform to watch the house, to make sure all you girls are safe. And for now, it's probably not safe for you to stay at the house." His eyes jumped around the room as he contemplated the next move.

"I'm not leaving that house! That house is my home, Reid. I will not let him drive me away from it the way he drove me away from my family. These girls are my family now. I've worked too hard to just turn and run now."

"But it's not safe there for you anymore. You'll come and stay at my place. The girls can look after everything until we find this guy."

"I'm not leaving the house!" Elandra said in a stern tone as she rose from her seat.

Kerith placed a hand on her arm. "But it's not safe there. You'll be safe at my place. I don't want you getting hurt." His voice took on a pleading tone.

"I'm not...wait, did you say your place?" Elandra asked in sudden confusion.

"Yes, now sit down."

Elandra sat back down and stared open-mouthed at him. "I'd stay at your place? Where would you be?"

"I'd be there with you, why wouldn't I be?" Kerith answered in a haze of his own confusion.

"I...I...well, that sounds great, but...but...I'm sorry, I just can't leave the house. That place means everything to me. It's my home, my work, my dream, my life..."

Kerith pushed a stray piece of hair behind Elandra's ear, "Okay, sweetie." He leaned forward and kissed her forehead. "We'll take care of this. I won't let him near you, okay?"

Elandra looked up into his eyes, her own misty with emotion, and she could only manage to nod her head.

"I'll take care of you, don't you worry."

Chapter 15

"And why are you so smiley?" Gen asked as Elandra closed the office door behind her.

Elandra leaned back against the door. "Hmm?" She felt as though she were in a dream.

"I asked what's got you in such a good mood." Gen smiled up at her. "It wouldn't have anything to do with that detective of yours, would it?"

"Well…" Elandra finally dropped her gaze down to Gen.

"Since when do you hold back from me?" Gen smirked.

Elandra rushed over and rolled a chair over beside Gen's desk. "He asked me to stay with him," she beamed.

"Like a weekend together or what? I need details, El."

"No, not a romantic weekend or anything. He said it would be safer if I stayed with him." Elandra smiled at the memory.

"Safer? What do you mean safer? Why would you need safer?" Gen's voice took on a sudden, anxious tone.

"What? Oh yeah." Elandra was awakened from her dreamlike state. "Someone broke in last night."

"What? Are you okay? Did anyone get hurt?"

"No, everyone is fine." Elandra felt a sudden ache in her stomach. *I can't tell Gen. She'd only worry and we have enough problems as it is. I can't burden her with this, she'll be safer if she doesn't know.* "No, everything is just fine. I'm pretty sure it was just a couple of punk kids doing it on a dare or something. They were gone when I came down to check out a noise."

"But you told Reid. So it had to be something," Gen prodded nervously.

"Well, I mean, obviously I was a bit shaken. So I called him this morning, and we got coffee. I just needed someone to tell me it was okay, you know. Just had to work out the wariness, and it worked. Telling Reid helped. It was no big deal." Elandra looked at Gen's worried expression. "Honestly, everything is fine. I promise."

"Okay. If you say so." Gen shifted papers nervously on her desk.

Elandra placed a hand on Gen's arm, stilling her movements. "Reid wouldn't let me back here if it wasn't okay."

Gen's shoulders fell as she let out a deep sigh. "You're right. Of course, you're right." She looked back up at Elandra and smiled. "You called Reid," she teased.

"Yeah, I did." Elandra blushed. "I didn't even think, I just picked up the phone and next thing I knew, I'd dialed him." Her blush turned an even deeper crimson.

"But you called Reid." Gen continued to tease.

"Yeah, I did." Elandra averted her gaze.

Gen laughed at Elandra's expression. "I've never seen you like this." She smiled wistfully. "Oh, honey, you're falling for him."

"Yeah, I think I am." She looked up at Gen, pure happiness shining in her eyes.

Gen reached around the table and squeezed Elandra in a tight hug. "Oh, El, I'm so happy for you. You deserve it, you really do." She pulled back. "After all those guys at Yale, you deserve it. I mean, those guys were slime. You deserve a good guy like Reid."

Elandra smiled sarcastically. "Yeah, Bradley was a complete jerk. He just wanted sex, and even then it was never good."

Gen rolled her eyes. "Or the short-lived Malcolm—Mister 'Equal.'" She did air quotes. "The one who alternated when you'd pay for dinner, saying it should be equal, like he was on the side of modern women." She snorted with disgust. "And then when it was his turn to pay, he'd take you to McDonald's and all the fast-food places, but only if it was a coupon day."

Elandra laughed. "But we can't forget Daniel." Elandra did her best impersonation of a nasal voice, pushing non-existent glasses up her nose. "I...I mean we can't forget..." Elandra snorted, "We can't forget about dear Daniel. The...the nice guy who was sure I'd make all his geek buddies jealous." She snorted again. "Treated me like a princess, but was more interested in my computer's hard drive than me, literally."

Gen burst out laughing. "Oh yeah, dear old Daniel: your attempt at finding a nice guy."

"Well he was nice," Elandra added, placing her hands up in defense, laughing the entire time.

"That he was. That he was." Gen continued to laugh.

The girls' laughter started to die down as they reminisced in the memories of their days at Yale. They smiled at their humble beginnings and sat in serene silence for a moment.

Then Gen's mood dropped. "I hate to rain on our happy parade, but what are we going to do about Mercedes, El?"

"I don't want to believe she's doing outside stuff, but after what I found out at the station yesterday, I just don't know." Elandra gave a deep sigh; her heart ached at the thought. *Mercedes can't be using us, none of my girls would ever do that. Oh please don't let it be true.*

"You went to the station?" Gen asked in confusion.

"Yeah, not long after I called you yesterday morning."

Gen cut her off, smiling. "From Reid's..." she teased.

"Yes." Elandra smiled. "After spending the night with Reid." She stuck her tongue out teasingly at Gen. "He got a call to go into work, and I went along, 'cause it was about Chloe."

"So what happened? Did you tell them what you found at Chloe's? Did you tell them about the senator?"

"I didn't have to. He was the reason Reid got called in. He came to volunteer the information that he met Chloe that night."

"So, he admitted being there, well that's something." Gen took in Elandra's sad expression. "Isn't it?"

Elandra shook her head. "Nope. He said that when he left, she was alive. And that's not even the worst part."

"There's something worse than losing a suspect?"

"Yeah. He admits that he paid Chloe for sex, and that he got her name from one of our girls."

Gen's face fell. "Oh, no."

"Yeah." Elandra sighed. "So that pretty much guarantees that Mercedes is doing extra work behind our backs."

"So what do we do about it?"

"I don't know. I just don't know." Elandra's shoulders fell in defeat. *It's not supposed to be like this, we took every precaution to avoid this.*

"Well we can't just come right out and accuse her. If she is as deep in as it seems, she'd just deny it, and then we'd be back at square one."

"Well, no matter what, we have to talk to her. Even if she denies it, we can at least listen to her defense." Elandra rose from her seat. "Come on. We might as well get this over with."

Chapter 16

Elandra and Gen headed off to the control room to wait for Mercedes to finish with a client. Elandra watched the screen with intense curiosity, trying to read more into Mercedes's moves than she was showing. She felt her heart ache at the idea of some of her girls selling themselves. *I created this place to be about real passion, real love, real romance.* Elandra sighed from the weight of her now heavy heart, and she crossed her arms, thinking it might hold her heart together.

"Do you think she does it to every guy?" Gen asked, looking at the middle screen biting a nail nervously.

The man sitting at the desk jerked around in his chair. "Does what?" he asked.

"Relax, Gerry," Elandra stated, making the technician blush. "We suspect Mercedes is doing extracurricular work with some of the clients."

Gerry perked up again. "Really?" He looked excitedly over at the screens.

"You can be such a pig sometimes, Gerry." Gen stuck her tongue out, teasing him.

"Sorry, Gerry. These would be outside the school, too," Elandra laughed.

"Oh." His shoulders and expression fell.

"Besides, that's what the cameras were mainly set up for—so we could ensure nothing like that was happening. So, no, we wouldn't have any of it on tape for you to take a close look at." Elandra smiled and winked at him.

Gerry's face turned a deep scarlet. "Uh, I wasn't thinking anything like that, girls." He looked up at them and put on his most innocent face. "Promise."

Both Gen and Elandra laughed.

"You know it's okay Gerry," Elandra said.

"Really?" he asked, the disbelief clearly written on his face.

"Well that is what the school is for," Elandra stated.

Gerry's eyes grew wide in astonishment. "To tape porn? 'Cause I'll be honest, some of you girls…" He gave a low wolf whistle. "Well, I'd buy those in a second."

Elandra laughed heartily. "I meant the cameras were to make sure the girls didn't sleep with any of the clients; this way we could protect the clients. So I'm afraid no porn was, is or will ever be made here. And since the school's goal is to find what turns certain men on, it's nice that you think we do a good job."

Gerry laughed off his embarrassment. "Well, that you do. You girls certainly know your jobs."

"She's heading out, El." Gen pointed at the screen.

"Thanks, Gerry." Elandra patted him on the back. "Enjoy the show." She smiled. "But not too much, 'cause if you make a mess, you have to clean it up," she teased.

The girls turned and left, leaving a scarlet-faced Gerry with his head in his hands, shaking in embarrassment.

Elandra casually left the control room, while Gen stormed her way out and up to Mercedes. Mercedes let the door quietly close behind her and turned to greet the girls.

"Hey, Elandra, Gen. What's up?" Her voice was calm and casual.

"Mercedes, are you doing extra work behind our backs?" Gen accused.

"I have no idea what you're talking about," Mercedes replied plainly.

"We…" Gen sputtered to a halt as Elandra silenced her with a wave of her hand.

"Mercedes, I'm worried about some of the things that happened with Chloe before she died." Elandra watched Mercedes expression intently. "I heard that you set up a meeting for Chloe the night she was killed."

"With the senator!" Gen burst in.

Elandra waved her silent again. "Do you remember our privacy agreement? The one we get you girls to all sign before you start working here?"

"Of course I remember it."

"Well, I have it under good authority that you set up a meeting for Chloe with one of our clients, and as you can remember from our agreement, that is strictly prohibited." Elandra placed herself in her best impersonation of a lawyer. "And as it stands, the person you set her up with just so happened to be a very prominent senator."

"That's right," Gen chimed in, her expression screaming *so there*.

"A senator? That doesn't sound familiar at all. I would never breach your trust, I swear it." Mercedes looked Elandra straight in the eye. "I swear."

Elandra watched Mercedes's eyes. "Are you sure?"

"Yeah." Mercedes nodded. "I never set Chloe up to meet anyone. Not one."

"Not even a Senator Prescott?" Elandra watched as Mercedes's eyes darkened in recognition of the name.

"Prescott…Prescott…wait a minute…" Mercedes hemmed and hawed, trying to buy time. "Now that I think about, I do remember setting a meeting up with Senator Prescott. Chloe said she knew him through her parents, and that she was hoping the senator could pass off a note to her father." She placed a hand on her waist. "That's right, I thought nothing of it. Why do you ask?"

"Well, when I was at the station, trying to help them gather info on Chloe, the senator was there with the police chief. He told the chief that he paid Chloe for sex."

"I just set the meeting up. Whatever Chloe did at it I have no knowledge of."

Elandra nodded as if agreeing, but in truth was assessing Mercedes's answers and responses.

"I figured since she told me she knew him before from being friends with her parents that it was an exception to the rule. I saw no harm in getting her in touch with someone she had told me was like an uncle to her," Mercedes said defensively.

"But you set the meeting up at a motel just off the highway? That seems a little out of the way and an odd choice of lodgings for the prominent senator," Elandra pointed out, watching Mercedes give the slightest of flinches.

"Hey, Senator Prescott told me that was where he was staying. He told me where she could meet him. I had nothing to do with that, and I don't like you implying I did," Mercedes barked back.

"I'm sorry if that's the way it came across." Elandra kept her tone calm and even. "I wasn't accusing you of anything."

"I was," Gen grumbled under her breath, earning her a glare from Mercedes and a warning look from Elandra.

"Well, is there anything else you can think of that can help the police out? I know you were Chloe's best friend, and I know this must be hard for you, but we need to find who did this," Elandra continued.

"No, I'm afraid I can't think of a thing."

"Well, thanks anyways, Mercedes. You let us know if you can think of anything, and we'll let you know when the cops catch the guy." Elandra smiled at her.

Gen raised an eyebrow in question at Elandra, recognizing Elandra's wolf smile. "Yeah, thanks, Mercedes."

"No problem." Mercedes turned to leave, but stopped a moment, turning back to Elandra. "Let me know if you want me to keep an eye on any of the other girls for signs of sex with clients."

"Thanks, Mercedes." Elandra once more flashed her wolf smile, and Mercedes smirked back, turned, and left.

Gen's head bolted over to look at Elandra. "All right, what the hell was that?" she huffed. "Why didn't we just come right out and say it? We knew she'd deny it anyways, so why no at least try to catch her off guard?"

"But we did catch her off guard," Elandra smirked.

"Excuse me?"

"Come on, Gen, 'I have no knowledge of it'? She had that rehearsed. It was obviously planned in case anyone caught wind of what was going on."

"What?"

"'That's where the senator said he was staying'? He decided the place?" Elandra sighed. "Oh Gen, think back to school. You didn't get that psych degree for nothing."

Gen shook her head. "Nope, I didn't see anything."

"Her pupils dilated at the mention of Senator Prescott, and she twitched when I brought up the motel."

"Then why didn't we just tell her we know?"

"Because it's not enough. Just 'cause she set up the meeting doesn't mean she killed Chloe."

"So what do we do now? Off to Kerith to see what we should do?" Gen asked.

"Yup, off to see the wizard, Dorothy." Elandra smiled and hooked her arm in Gen's.

"So does this make me? Watson?" Gen smiled as they walked down the hall.

"I think of me more as Nancy Drew, and that makes you either Bess or George. You've got a choice, unless of course you want to be both of the Hardy Boys."

"I won't be a Hardy Boy, but I will have one." Gen winked.

"Okay." The girls laughed. "But as Nancy, I get first dibs."

"What? No way. You have Kerith, and that means I get both boys." The girls burst into laughter and continued down the hall.

Chapter 17

He knelt in front of the stone and placed his meager bouquet of flowers down before it. He touched the stone lovingly, closed his eyes, and let the well of emotions he was feeling flow into it. He brought his hand back, laid them both in his lap, and looked up at the face that was etched into the stone.

"I'm early this year, Marie." He smiled. "I have news for you. I found her, Marie. Remember the girl I told you about, the one all those years ago? I've found her again. And this time, I won't let her go." He took a deep breath. "Do you remember our story, Marie? Do you remember what you did for me?

"As my mother's attending nurse, you stole me away. You and my doctor were in love, but due to hospital regulations, you couldn't get married. And you lived, without the church and without the law, as if the two of you were married. And due to a medical condition you couldn't bear children, so when you realized my mother was having twins, you saw an opportunity. My mother could only afford to raise one child, so when Michael told her she was only having one she was ecstatic. So without her even knowing, you stole me away right after birth and then raised me as your own. Marie, you were the best mother I could ever ask for."

The crunching of the grass behind him warned him of the coming presence before the hand even touched his shoulder. "We have to go, Jacob; everything is falling into place. It's time we go and watch it unfold." The guest turned and started to walk away.

Jacob rose and looked down at the tombstone, "Happy birthday, Marie. I shall always remain your son."

*

She swiveled her hips, danced her way over to the bed, and hopped on. She pulled the upside-down spoon out of her mouth. "Tell me a secret, Carter."

He reached toward the spoon, and she jerked it back, clutching the ice-cream tub to her chest. She made a sound of disapproval. "Get your own," she pouted.

He pulled a spoon out from under his pillows. "Nope. You get to share this time." He dug his spoon in.

She continued to pout, but went on eating. "So, tell me a secret."

He sat up and pulled her up beside him, hugging her to his side as they continued to eat. "Well, pretty soon I'll be able to buy you all the ice cream you want."

She raised an eyebrow at him in question. "All my own? No sharing?"

He kissed her nose. "No sharing."

"Well that's not much of a secret." She pouted even further.

"The ice cream isn't the secret," he replied.

"It isn't?" she asked coyly.

He shook his head. "Nope. The secret is where I get the money from."

"Where's that?"

"I've got an account in the Cayman Islands. You know the fundraising board I'm on for the children's hospital?" She nodded her head, and he continued, "Well I'm not just fundraising for them, I'm also fundraising for me." He placed another spoonful in his mouth. "And pretty soon I'll have enough to buy everything I want. I can take you on as my own personal concubine, and I can buy you all the ice cream you want. Hell, I'll buy you a whole rocky-road factory if you want." He smirked down at her.

She stared at him in wonderment and was snapped out of it when cold ice cream dripped onto her.

"Oh…" She pouted looking down at her chest.

He stopped her hand from wiping it up and leaned forward, licking it off. He took the ice-cream tub from her hand and placed it and the spoons on the nightstand. He kissed his way across her shoulder and up her neck, and they tumbled down onto the bed together. They rolled back and forth until he was on top, and in one swift move, he plunged deep into her.

They moaned in unison, and he groaned her name, "Mercedes…"

Chapter 18

"Listen, Kerith, you need this one. I talked to the guys over at recruitment, and they want to meet you, but you need to prove yourself. I've given you a glowing recommendation, and your record speaks for itself, but you could really use this one." The chief looked over at Kerith. "This could be a really great opportunity for you, and I don't want to see anything ruin that."

"You mean Elandra?" Kerith questioned in a stern voice, not looking at the other man.

"Yes. Look I know you like her, Kerith, but…well, I just don't think she's right."

"She doesn't run a whorehouse, you know." Kerith continued to keep his gaze averted.

"I know, but she has a funny past."

"You checked up on her?" Kerith's head shot up in anger.

"Of course I did." He placed a hand up, stopping Kerith's oncoming rage. "And before you ask, it was for the case, not just because of you. That school of hers is clean, but she may not be. She changed her name a few years back, I couldn't find any witness protection or anything, but she changed it."

"I know," Kerith added calmly.

"What? You knew?"

"Yeah, she had a stalker a while back, and he threatened her family, so to protect them, she changed her name and left home."

The chief ran a hand through his thinning hair. "Jesus, Kerith. What have you gotten yourself into?" He shook his head, looking concerned.

"The stalker had raped her first."

The chief's face dropped. "Holy shit."

"Yeah." Kerith leaned back in his seat and crossed his arms.

"You know I'm just worried about you. I don't want to see you get into anything too messed up. You had enough with Stephanie; you need someone without issues now." He blew out a deep breath. "I just don't want you to fall for the wrong girl, and I think this Elandra is wrong."

Kerith looked over at the man who had been like a father and wished he understood. "I know you're concerned, but your warnings come a little late."

"Ah Jesus, Kerith," the chief moaned.

They paused, listening to banging from down the hall and watched the door, expecting answers. The door collapsed open, and Gen and Elandra fell into the office.

"What the hell?" muttered Chief Phillip. "Oh. It's you," he added upon spotting Elandra.

"Chief…" Kerith glared at him, rising from his seat.

The girls stood up, straightening themselves, and Elandra glared at the chief. "Listen, if you don't like me, that's fine. But you're going to have to at least deal with me for now," Elandra snapped, "because we have an idea who it was that killed my Chloe."

"Oh you do, do you?" The chief leaned back in his chair. "Fancy yourself Sherlock, do we? Did you hear that, Reid, your girlfriend thinks she's Sherlock Holmes."

"Don't patronize me." Elandra's glare turned ever icier. "If anything, I'm Nancy Drew." She smirked at him, earning herself a quick chortle from the chief, which was silenced by Kerith. "And besides, I don't think it's any of your business if Reid and I are seeing each other." All movement and sound in the room came to a grinding halt.

"Excuse me?" The chief returned Elandra's glare.

She leaned forward, resting her palms on his desk. "You can sit there and huff and puff all you want. But the matter is, you're just the big bad wolf, and you can't blow down this house. Reid and I are together, and whether you like it or not, we're going to stay that way. Now you can either congratulate him, or you can avoid dealing with me altogether, it's your choice. But for now…" She stood back up, crossing her arms. "…you get to help us figure out what to do about one of my employees who is selling off my girls."

Chief Phillip looked like a solid stone volcano that was about to explode, but all of a sudden, he burst out in laughter. "Well I really didn't think you had it in you." He rose from his chair and stretched out his hand to Elandra. "Kerith, here, is like a son to me, and I was worried you'd never have it in you to put up a fight. But goddammit, girl, you got spirit, I'll give you that." He smiled, shaking Elandra's hand. "This boy needs a strong woman to keep him in line, and I believe you will." He resumed his seat, looking thoroughly pleased with himself. "I like ya, girlie, so there's no worries there. I just wasn't sure if you were right for my boy here." He shook his head and laughed to himself.

Kerith stood, open-mouthed, staring at the chief. "You're kidding me."

"Nope, you've done good for yourself, Reid. Now…" He looked back at Elandra and Gen. "…what's this about prostitution?"

Elandra shook herself back to reality. "Right."

"Well it's like this, chief—" Gen started until she was waved off by Elandra.

"Not quite, Watson. My show." She stuck her tongue out teasingly.

"Oh fine, but next time it's my turn," Gen teased back.

"Girls, I don't exactly have all day. Trying to catch a killer here, remember?"

"Right, sorry. Okay, The night I was attacked, I had been at Chloe's apartment. While there I found her schedule. It said that she was to meet the senator." She was cut off.

"We know that, Miss Rosedale," the chief added.

"Elandra, please," she corrected.

"Fine, but please, time is an element."

"Right. Well I also found a phone message from one of my employees, Mercedes. The message told me that Mercedes was the one that set up the meeting with the senator." She watched the chief nod his head in understanding. "So we, Gen and I, took it upon ourselves to ask Mercedes a few questions." She held up her hand to stop the chief. "Yes, you're going to say we should have left it to you boys. Well you don't have the training we do, and you don't know her enough to know her tells. She reacted to the senator's name, which is no surprise considering that, after we mentioned who Chloe met, she just so happened to remember setting the meeting up. She also flinched at the mention of the motel, and she used choice phrases that wouldn't be someone's first reaction when being questioned about a murder. The senator had started out as working with Mercedes, so there was that connection. Mercedes is too smart to admit to anything, but I know her well enough to be able to read when she's into something she shouldn't be. And this is like a screaming billboard." The chief had his hands folded together and was considering them for a moment, so Elandra finished, "So that's why we came to you. We're not sure what to do next."

"You're sure Mercedes is the one setting it all up?" The chief closed his eyes in thought.

"I don't like to say it, but yeah, I'm sure of it," Elandra sighed.

"We both are, sir," Gen added in.

The chief opened his eyes and drew himself up to his desk. "All right, what we need is some record of her setting it up. The senator isn't enough; we need more. We need someone to play bait. Reid, I want you in. I want you to be a new student and get her to play Madame." He clicked the intercom on his desk, in full business mode. "Reilly, get your ass in here." He looked back at them and waited until Reilly entered the room.

"Yeah, chief?"

"I want you in with them. We need the techies to hook Reid up to be monitored: audio, and even visual if we can. I want—"

He was cut off by Elandra. "We have cameras."

"I'm sorry?" the chief asked, faltering.

"We have cameras at the school. They're supposed to ensure the girls don't cross the decency line," Elandra explained, expecting a reprimand from the chief.

"They got audio?" he asked.

Elandra shook herself in shock. "Yes, of course."

"Perfect." He looked back at Reilly. "I still want you to go with them. I want Reid in trying to snake this girl." He looked back Elandra. "I am afraid to say that we did suspect something like this after my first meeting with you." He ignored Elandra's incredulous look. "We started to suspect that someone from your school had taken over Becky's clients after she was killed, But now we know—"

He was cut off again by Elandra. "I'm sorry, I must be missing something. It was Chloe who was killed. What are you talking about with some Becky?"

The chief looked over at Kerith, who was staring intently at the ground. He muttered, "She was my sister."

"Sister?" Elandra whispered.

"She was a hooker," Reilly added calmly.

Kerith glared over at him.

"What? Sorry Reid, but she was."

Kerith sighed, "Yeah."

"You're sister was a hooker?" Gen asked in shock.

"Yeah. She...she worked a lot of politicians." Kerith admitted.

"Major politicians." Reilly added, nodding—earning him an even darker glare from Kerith.

"Reid, just get it over with. Either you share with the ladies, or I will," the chief threatened.

Kerith took a deep breath and ploughed through the pain. "Becky played hooker to some major politicians when they came into town. Only...only that wasn't what she was really after. Becky was a smart girl, and she wanted bigger and better. She'd get them comfortable with her, and then she'd ask them questions. She'd get them to tell her campaign secrets, anything, everything that congress, the law, and especially the public would look down upon. She'd get them to share info, and then she'd blackmail them— take everything she could from them. She did very well for herself; that is until she found out the wrong person's secrets. If you remember a few years back, there was speculation about a certain politician having connections to the mob. Well, Becky found out it was true. But when she tried to blackmail him, he retaliated with putting a hit on her. Though it couldn't and probably never will be proved, Becky was killed by the mob for trying to swindle the wrong politician, along with an innocent bystander who was trying to help Becky get out of the life."

"Oh, Reid." Elandra walked over to Kerith and hugged him close. She pulled back and looked up at him, a tear running down her cheek. "I'm sorry about your sister."

The chief cleared his throat and rose from his seat. "We gotta set things in motion. I want this girl in tonight."

Reilly's back straightened, "Right, chief."

Kerith hugged Elandra close again and kissed her forehead. "Thanks," he whispered to her.

"Come on guys." The chief herded them all toward the door, "I want this wrapped up and finished tonight."

Everyone started filing out the door when the chief placed a hand on Kerith's back, stalling his exit. "Don't let her go, Kerith." The chief patted him on the back and winked as he watched them head out the door.

Chapter 19

Kerith walked cautiously into the room, trying to absorb every detail before he would have to focus on the task at hand. Elandra had filled him in on the basic setup of the school's lessons, but it was always the individuals involved that kept the scenarios fresh and unpredictable. He wandered aimlessly around the room, wondering when Mercedes would join him and what he should do in the meantime. He stared over at the partition; Elandra hadn't told him what was on the other side. She had said he wouldn't reach that point in the lesson.

*

"He needs to relax. He needs to stop shifting around the room like that." Reilly paced in the control room. "He looks nervous. She'll know something is up if he keeps fluttering around."

Gen giggled, and Elandra smiled at Reilly. "Actually, this is part of our technique," she explained to Reilly as if he were a clueless seven-year-old. "We always play a waiting game the first meeting. It keeps them guessing;

wondering what's going to happen. It puts their senses and emotions on high alert." She watched as Reilly started to bite at his nails as Kerith paced. "If he didn't have this reaction, then we'd be in trouble. Reid needs to be kept in the dark and on edge, just like a new student would be. The girls are trained to read body movements and emotions. Mercedes would know something was going on if Kerith didn't react like a new student. So believe me when I say it's better that he is nervous."

*

Kerith crossed to the partitioned barrier and stopped dead in his tracks. A bed. There was a bed in the room. Kerith numbly walked up to it like a zombie, and his hand reached out to the sheets. Silk.

"Jesus Christ," he swore under his breath as he strode back to the partition.

No wonder Elandra hadn't warned me about this side. This is for the part of the lesson that includes the girlfriend or wife, or even the prostitute, he thought. With Elandra watching, this definitely wasn't the side he wanted to use—at least not without Elandra instead of some political hooker. Kerith stared at the bed, his breath quickening as he pictured himself with Elandra in the room. He rested his hand on the partition, needing to keep himself upright. Kerith started to picture all the things he could do to Elandra on that bed. He pictured his hands running down her body, then spreading her out before him. He pictured himself kissing his way up each of her legs, giving but a whisper's touch to the area where she craved him most. Kerith's breath became heavy and labored as he pictured her squirming, withering, and begging him to touch her where she needed him most. Kerith felt his free hand clenching in anticipation, his whole body tense and focused on his fantasy. Just as he was picturing his mouth moving in to lick, suck, and nip at Elandra's very core, he heard the soft click of the door. He turned to meet the new guest and had to do a double-take at the vision that stood before him.

"Miss Mercedes?" he inquired meekly.

She snapped her gum, "Yeah, so what?"

"Um…" Kerith was unsure what to do next. "I'm Clayton, um, Clayton Thomas," he stuttered, trying to appear shy.

"Yeah. So what am I to do about it?" She cracked her gum again.

"I'm sorry. This, uh, this was a…a mistake," he jabbered, making as if to leave.

Her manner became sweet as candy in a split second. "Oh, no, honey, sorry." She giggled. "El told me you needed a firm hand." She giggled some more. "Said you need someone who'll push you to test your limits. But don't worry, being your first time, we'll go slow and at your pace. Okay?"

"Oh…okay," he stammered.

"Here, sweetie, have a seat." She gestured to the café table and pair of chairs. "I'll explain everything first, how's that?"

Kerith nodded mildly as he sat down. "That…that would be great. Thanks."

She pulled out the chair across from him and sat down. "You know, you look kind of familiar; have we met before?" she asked, arching a brow.

Kerith's mind raced and snapped into action, "No, no, I…I don't think…don't think so." He averted his gaze. "I'd...I'd remember...remember you." He smiled up at her. "But they...they say that...that everyone has... has a dopp...a doppelganger some...somewhere in...in the world."

She smiled at him. "Well, my name is Mercedes. Don't worry about no *Miss* or anything. Just call me Mer, or we can use a different name when we come to the actual scenario if you want. But Mer will do for now." She smiled kindly at him.

"Th...thanks. I'm Clayton Thomas." He nodded. "S...sorry about this."

"Oh, no need, sweetie. First-timers are always nervous." She placed a hand over top of his on the table. "Why don't we just talk and get to know each other a bit first, how's that sound?"

"Oh...okay." He pulled his hand back shyly.

"Why don't you tell me a bit about yourself, Clayton?"

"Well, I'm...I'm not normally this shy. It's just...just when...when I'm...I'm with a beau...beau...when I'm with a beautiful woman," he forced himself to spit out.

Mercedes smiled at him. "Well, that's very sweet of you to say. Thank you," she said, urging him to continue.

Kerith swiped at his brow as though this were causing him great stress. "Well, I'm...I'm normally a pol... politician. I...I work with the congress in Washington. So...so normally I'm actually very...very assertive." He smiled up at her meekly.

Mercedes eyes lit up at the word *politician*. "A politician. Well, I can certainly see you standing up for the people's rights." Her smile was like that of a vulture starting to circle around their prey. You work in Washington, did you say?"

Kerith made himself appear to ease with familiar ground. "Yes. I work with the congress. I do, however, make frequent stops here on my political journey."

"Frequent? Well then perhaps we'll see much of each other." She smiled like a fox, calculating and planning.

Kerith straightened his back, making his words more sure. "Yes. Yes, perhaps we will."

"Do you enjoy your job? I see it as one where you're constantly changing job description," she chuckled.

"Well I'm certainly moving up in the field. I'm hoping somewhere down the line that I can..." He chuckled. "...'Get into bed' with the right politician and hopefully run for vice president," he finished, adding air quotes.

"Vice president?" Mercedes's eyes darkened, "Well you certainly do have high hopes, don't you?" she cooed. "But I can see you're more relaxed. Feeling better now? More at ease?"

"Oh yes, quite. Thank you."

"Well, we have two options now, really. We could dive right in, and I could teach you to harness your lust, or we can simply spend this lesson explaining. I can explain what will happen with your time here at Hidden Desires." She smiled up at him from under hooded eyes. "With some, diving right in works, but I have a feeling that you might need to have a better idea about what we really do here. But the choice is up to you: which would you like?"

"Why don't you explain this time? I'm a little worried that if we try to dive right in, I'll shrink back again and become the nervous boy I was in high school."

*

"Hmm…" Elandra mused.

"What? Something wrong?" Reilly continued to watch the screen but addressed Elandra.

"Well, we do let students choose what happens the first lesson; we like to let them feel as though they are in charge of how far things go. But…" She stroked her chin in thought. "…we make it a habit never to suggest what they choose. That takes the power away."

"So you think…" He turned to face her. "You think this is a sign of her crossing other boundaries, too?"

"Probably. I mean, she's too interested. We never ask in-depth questions about their jobs or intimate details of their life. We find a safe topic they feel comfortable talking about; we don't get personal, so that we can protect their privacy."

"She's getting too close to him," Gen added, looking over at Elandra. The two exchanging worried glances.

*

"Well, each of us plays a part. You're a visual learner with a little kinesthetic aspect as well, so you mainly get something from things that are visually stimulating but also a little hands-on. So in here, you play a customer at the café, and I play the snide New York waitress. The waitress gives you the visual stimulation, with its gestures and mannerisms, while the New York attitude is brash and directly pushes you to test your limits. I play someone who is so intensely 'in your face' that it forces you to react. I push your boundaries, and you act purely by impulse, and it's that impulse we're trying to teach you to get at; that primal hunger and lust for another person. So, did you want to test a little bit of it out? I think you're ready." She winked at him.

"Sure." He smiled up at her as she rose from her seat and walked across to a hidden closet.

Kerith noticed she looked the part; shoulder-length, straight, blonde hair, tight white T-shirt hugging her curves with some catchy phrasing imprinted across the chest, jeans that had been cut roughly into shorts, and high-top sneakers. She snapped her gum with attitude, wrapped a waitress apron around her waist, and grabbed a pad of paper from the pocket. *She looks like New York Barbie with Bronx attitude,* Kerith thought.

She wandered back to the table where he lazed back in his chair. "What d'ya want?" she asked, taking on a perfect New York accent.

"How about a coffee." Kerith smirked, "And a waitress with a better attitude. too."

Mercedes's head jerked up. "Wise ass, eh? You have a problem with the service, you can always go somewhere else." She sneered at him and added, "Sir."

Kerith chuckled softly, "No I think I'll stay right where I am." He hooked his arm over the back of the chair. "Any bad service will be reflected in the tip."

Mercedes playfully glared back at him. "Well, I can always reserve my right to refuse service."

"No can do, sweetheart. You see, I happen to be good friends with the owner." He smiled smugly.

Mercedes snuffed, "So what, you expect me just to do as you say? I think not."

"Oh, you'll do exactly as I tell you, and as a matter of fact, you'll enjoy doing everything I tell you." He smiled up at her, feeling himself getting lost in the role. "And I mean *everything* I tell you."

Mercedes's eyes darkened with silent pleasure, and she felt herself growing warm with anticipation and desire. "You sure about that?"

Kerith's legs fell open as he relaxed even deeper into the role. "You bet I am."

"Well then, I guess I best give you my undivided attention." She threw the pad and pencil onto the table and walked toward him. "And make sure that I fulfill all your pleasures." She stepped forward and positioned herself over his lap so that her waist was at his eye level. "And believe me when I say, I will definitely love every minute I spend making you happy and doing exactly as I'm told." She lowered herself onto his lap, anchoring her legs on either side of his.

*

Elandra's face burned red with rage, and she turned, ready to storm into the other room. Just as her hand reached the doorknob, Reilly grabbed Elandra by the waist, halting her from flying from the room.

"This is where the scenario ends and where the girlfriend or wife is supposed to take over," Elandra ground out.

"We need to let them finish. We have nothing definite yet."

Elandra glared at him. "She's sitting on his lap, what more do you want?"

"We have no way of knowing that that's not part of your lesson plan."

"What? You arrogant, son of a…" Elandra spat.

"El." Gen pointed back at the screen, directing Elandra's attention to the newly unfolding drama.

*

Kerith gulped back the lump in his throat. "I guess you better," he squeaked out, clearing his throat and returning his voice to its usual timbre. "Yeah, I guess you better."

Mercedes's eyes fixed on his and drew him deeper into the fantasy. "Why don't we move somewhere more comfortable then?" Her voice was like velvet, wrapping itself around Kerith.

She stood up and reached back into the closet, flipped on a radio and turned the volume up. She gently took his hand in hers and led him across the room. As they went, she looked back at him over her shoulder, smiling seductively and pushing Kerith to the point where he fell entirely into the fantasy, forgetting the outside world. She led him over to the bed and gently pushed him back onto it, climbing on and straddling his lap. She ran her hands up and down his chest, pausing at the top and slowly undoing the buttons of his shirt.

"You know, Clayton, if you visit our little town often on your political journey, then I could always keep you company," she cooed, and she pushed open his shirt and gasped at his broad chest and defined muscles.

Kerith's mind shook as he fell back to reality, remembering what he was doing and what he was suppose to be doing. "You mean come to the school?" he asked, trying to regain his control.

"Not just the school. I could, you know, be your special friend." She leaned down and kissed his chest.

Kerith groaned, fighting to remember what was happening. "Special friend? I...I already have a girlfriend."

"Oh, no, I don't mean date." She nipped at his chest. "I mean we could get together every time you're in town. You know." She raised her head, looking deep into his eyes. "I could be there for any time you need to work out some kinks."

"Kinks?" he squeaked and cleared his throat again. "Kinks?" His voice returned to normal.

Mercedes giggled, "You're so cute and innocent. What I mean is that, whenever you come to town, we can fuck like rabbits." Her laugh deepened with desire. "I have very reasonable rates, and I work with a lot of people from Washington." She leaned down and kissed his chest again. "Though I'm sure you and I can work out a better deal." Her hands moved to his belt, and she slowly started to undo it. "I mean, I think I would enjoy working with you as much as you would with me." She lowered her head again and started kissing her way down his body.

Suddenly the room was bombarded with a sea of noise as three bodies fell through the door.

Chapter 20

Mercedes jumped. "What the hell is going on here?"

Reilly strode up to her. "Place your hands behind your back. You're under arrest for prostitution—"

Mercedes cut him off. "What?" Her head jerked over to Elandra. "You! You stupid bitch! How could you do this to me?" she screamed.

"Me? You were supposed to be Chloe's best friend!" Elandra screamed back, her blood boiling.

"Ha, that's a laugh. I was never her best friend; Chloe was just the perfect in. Political parents. She was a complete and willing idiot. She knew people I could never dream of getting as clients." Mercedes laughed, "Chloe was simply a means to an end."

"A means to an end?" Elandra raged. "You used her!"

"Oh, I used more than just her." Mercedes smirked, but it suddenly disappeared into anger. "And if that stupid bitch, Chloe, hadn't gone and got herself killed, then it would have continued, and none of you would have had a clue."

"Don't be stupid, Mercedes. We were onto you." Elandra ground her teeth.

"Come on, Elandra, did you really think we kept all those clients by just arousing them?" Mercedes laughed. "You're so naïve. It was so easy to work through the school, and no one was the wiser. I mean, I pulled had my clients during 'school hours.'" Mercedes cackled, "A little music, a strategically thrown blanket and I had them in this very house. And you knew nothing!"

"You mean, you didn't just recruit some of the girls or seduce some of the students? You...you..." Elandra couldn't bring herself to say it.

"I played political hooker in this house, right under your very nose." Mercedes sneered.

Kerith watched Elandra's face heat with anger, and he nodded his head at Reilly. Reilly stepped forward and placed the cuffs on Mercedes's wrists.

Reilly snapped the cuffs shut, and Mercedes just sneered. "No judge will ever find me guilty. I have clients come all the way from Washington. I know so many political secrets no one would dare sentence me. They all know that, if I was ever found out, then with a mere slip of my tongue, the whole world would know their precious secrets."

Reilly nudged her toward the door. "Come on, Kerith. You grab the tape, and we'll take her in."

"Kerith?" Mercedes stopped mid-step and glared back at Kerith. "You son of a bitch." She spat, "You're the cop who was asking questions after Chloe's death. I knew I recognized you." Her eyes bore into Kerith. "What was the last name again?"

Elandra stepped up and wrapped her arms around Kerith's waist. "Reid." Kerith hugged her close.

Mercedes scoffed, "That's right. I have your sister to thank for my very lucrative business." She paused for a moment in thought, watching Elandra and Kerith cling to each other. "Becky wasn't alone the night she was killed, though, if I remember correctly." She sneered at Elandra. "You should ask Kerith about the other victim." Mercedes smirked, proud of herself. "Why don't you ask him about Stephanie?"

Kerith's entire body tensed in rage, "Shut up, Mercedes."

"Come on, Elandra, he's had to have told you about his beloved Stephanie," she jeered.

Reilly pushed his elbow into Mercedes's back, "Come on, you."

Elandra withdrew herself from Kerith's embrace. "Who's Stephanie?"

"Yeah, who's Stephanie?" Gen glared at Kerith.

Mercedes cackled once more, causing Reilly to push her toward the door. "Come on, it's best we leave them alone." Reilly grabbed Gen's arm and dragged her and Mercedes out the door.

*

Elandra waited until the door closed behind them before she turned and glared at Kerith. "Mind explaining what that was about? And who's Stephanie?" she growled.

Kerith raised his hands up in defense, "Whoa, okay, before you go violent on my ass, let me explain."

Elandra crossed her arms, feeling her anger now being directed toward Kerith. "By all means, explain."

Kerith raked a hand through his hair and blew out a deep breath. "Okay, it goes like this:" He started pacing around the room. "Back when Becky was working the politicians, me and Stephanie learned about it early. At that point I was just a newbie, so I didn't want to risk my whole career with family crap that I wasn't even involved in. So instead of just turning her over to the cops, Stephanie and I decided to try to work with Becky to get her out of the biz. I mean no guy wants to learn that their baby sister is a hooker. I had always protected her and...and..." He stopped and turned to face Elandra. "Well, I felt like I had failed her." When Elandra's expression didn't change, he continued his pacing. "I felt that it was my fault she was in that life, and so I...well, I wanted to fix it. I wanted to fix her." Kerith's movements were jilted and erratic; he took another deep breath, trying to calm his words. "I knew that I couldn't fix everything on my own, so I asked Stephanie to help me. I knew I couldn't help as much and not put my work at risk, so it was Stephanie that did most of the pushing and struggling with Becky. She was a real angel about it. She never complained about helping out once." His eyes glazed over with memory. "But when Becky got into deep trouble with the mob, it was Stephanie who worked out a plan to get Becky someplace safe. Stephanie was working to get Becky out of the state and, well, just hidden." He stopped pacing and faced Elandra again, looking dead serious. "So when they came after Becky, well...well, Stephanie got in their way. The mob had too much at risk, and they weren't about to let Becky talk. Which meant they also weren't about to let anything get in their way. The night they found her, Stephanie and Becky were just packing the last of her things to get her out of town. Becky tried to promise them that she'd never breath a word, and that she'd as good as forget ever meeting the guy, but they wouldn't accept it. They said it was easier and safer for them just to get rid of her. So when Stephanie tried to reason with them, well they figured she knew too much, and that she'd have to go, too." He paused, and his eyes shot down to the ground. "The next morning, we found them in Becky's apartment. They'd each been shot through the back of the head, like an execution. Everyone knew what had happened, but no one had the nerve to say anything. It was shut down as unsolvable and basically thrown in the back of the closet. No one even wanted to try to give them justice."

Elandra listened to the anger in his voice grow—there had been no justice. Two girls would never be put to rest because everyone was too scared to even try. Elandra felt her heart ache for the girls and for the pain Kerith had had to go through on his own.

"No one cared. I guess they felt that Becky had deserved it. But Stephanie…Stephanie didn't deserve it—not that." He shoved his hands into his pockets and continued to stare at the ground.

Elandra remembered then why she was hearing this story. "I'm sorry about what happened to your sister, I really am. But that doesn't explain who Stephanie is. Or why Mercedes brought her up." She sighed and felt her entire body tense as she squeezed the next words out. "It also doesn't explain why Mercedes called her your beloved."

Kerith's gaze shifted back up to Elandra, and his anger disappeared, "You might want to sit for this one." He motioned to one of the chairs.

"I'm fine standing, thank you," she clipped.

He blew out a deep breath and pulled the opposite chair out for himself. "Stephanie was my fiancée."

The news hit Elandra like a brick being thrown at her stomach. "Fi...fiancée?" she squeaked out. She leaned on the back of the chair in front of her.

"Yeah. And...well, the night before her and Becky were murdered..." Kerith tried to press all his haunted memories and emotions down, so he could explain it all to her. "I had actually just proposed to Stephanie the night before they were killed."

"Oh." Elandra gripped the chair so hard her knuckles turned white. "I see." She walked around on wobbly knees and collapsed into the chair.

Kerith shifted his head down, trying to look into her eyes, but they were lost and clouded. "Elandra?"

"I...I think..." Elandra cleared her throat, trying to get a hold of herself. "I think you need to go now."

"Elandra, there's more." He leaned forward in his seat, drew a deep breath, and seeing that she wasn't going to raise her gaze, continued on. "The morning that they were killed, Stephanie told me she was pregnant. We were celebrating our engagement the night before, so she wanted it to be a surprise so we could celebrate all over again. I was going to have a kid. I was going to have the type of family I had always wanted." His gaze drifted to the side, and he smiled, lost in the memories.

Elandra lifted her head to look up at him, tears brimming in her eyes, as she listened to the joy in his voice. She watched as his face fell again into tortured despair. She felt her soul ache for him and had to turn her eyes away from the pain.

Kerith let out a rough sigh. "I've never told anyone that. No one else knows that she was pregnant. We hadn't gotten the chance to tell anyone." He looked up, unable to see Elandra's threatening tears. "Since the whole thing was hushed up, no autopsy was ever done, so the case file doesn't even show that there were really three deaths that morning." He sighed. "Look, I honestly thought I was in love with her. But…but now…now I think maybe it was just comfort. You know, Stephanie and I had reached that point where we were perfectly comfortable together, and it was like…I don't know. It just seemed like the thing to do and that…that made me think I was doing it out of love. But…but now I know it wasn't. What I felt for Stephanie wasn't love, I can say that for sure, because I didn't know what love was until now." Elandra's hurt eyes, glistened with unshed tears as she looked up at him. "I didn't know until I met you. I…I love you, Elandra. I love you, and now that this is all over, we can be together. It is perfect, you can leave Hidden Desires, you don't need to run this place anymore. We can get married, start a family and I can look after you. You can get a real job if you want, you don't need other men looking and touching you like they do here. We can start a proper life together." Kerith reached out his arm to touch her, but pulled back before he came an inch from her. "Elandra?"

Elandra felt her heart drop as she heard the words play over in her head. He had a fiancée and a child, her mind whispered, but then the rest of his words sunk in. *Leave*

Hidden Desires, a proper life, her mind screamed at her. "Proper life? What the hell does that mean?"

Kerith looked shocked by her question, "I mean you don't need to work here anymore. You don't have to be a sex object to men."

Her chest tightened, "Sex object? You... you still think this is a whorehouse. I can't believe you! This is my life's work, this school is my pride and joy. I would never leave it."

"But you don't have to work with the men, you could get a respectable job."

Elandra's world was consumed in pain, "Please, Kerith. It's best if you go."

Kerith's shoulders fell in defeat, "Okay." He whispered and rose from his seat. "If...if you need anything, just give me a call, okay?" he asked, trying desperately to reach her.

Elandra didn't respond. She simply turned her head to the side so he couldn't see the pain in her eyes. Kerith headed toward the door and paused with it in his hand. He looked back at Elandra and knew that there was nothing he could do for her; nothing he could do for them. He had to let the information sink in, and all he could do was wait—wait and hope. Without saying another word, Kerith turned and let the door swing silently closed behind him.

Elandra felt as though her head were swimming and she could gather no clear thoughts. Her heart ached and broke in two. She felt her world collapse and felt herself fall apart. She leaned forward on the table and buried her face in her arms. It was only then that she let the waterfall of tears start to fall.

Chapter 21

Elandra bid the couple before her good-bye and returned to shuffling the schedule to account for the loss of Chloe. Gen walked up behind her and reached under Elandra's arms to the old calendar. She had kept silent the past week, not asking Elandra what had happened, but it took all her strength not to push Elandra for details. Gen turned to leave, but was stopped by the sound of the opening door.

"I've got a delivery for a Miss Rosedale?" came the voice behind a large bouquet of flowers.

The owner of the voice shuffled his way in and placed the flowers into the cradle of his arm. As he surveyed the place, Elandra and Gen rated the delivery guy. Sandy blond hair, surfer-toned body, about twenty-five, and face filled with an awe-struck, innocent look. Nice house, but nobody's home; Elandra thought.

"Can we help you?" Elandra asked, gazing at the wide-eyed guppy holding the flowers.

"Uh, yeah. Are you guys like, a prostitute house or something?" he asked in amazement.

Elandra gave a little growl of frustration. "No! Now what do you want?" she clipped.

Gen tsked her with a look as she stepped toward the delivery guy. "What she means is, can we help you deliver the flowers?" She smiled.

"What? Oh yeah." He shook his wonder off. "They're for a Miss Rosedale." He checked his clipboard.

"I didn't order any flowers," Elandra squeezed out in a hiss through pursed lips.

Gen glared back at Elandra. "Here, allow me." She reached forward and took the flowers from him. "Let me just sign for these." She passed the flowers to Elandra and took the clipboard.

Gen quickly signed her John Hancock and ushered the poor delivery boy out the door. She closed it behind him with a snap and returned to Elandra's side.

"All right, El, who are these from? I mean you couldn't even be nice to the little side dish," Gen chided.

"He thought we were a whorehouse." Elandra ground her teeth.

"Still no reason to bite off his head. And it's not just him; you've been in a foul mood ever since Mercedes was arrested. Now I know something happened with Kerith, and I've been doing my best not to push, But, well, honey, you've gotten to be pretty impossible to be around."

Elandra's shoulders sagged, and she sighed, "I know. I'm sorry Gen, it's just…just…" she drew a deep breath and tumbled her way through her next words. "Reid and I didn't end on a good note."

"Well, who would have guessed?" Gen teased.

Elandra chuckled softly, but Gen still felt her sad tension.

"So who sent the flowers?" Gen asked, trying to lighten the mood. She reached across Elandra and quickly stole the card. "Hmm…" Her expression gave way to one of puzzlement. "There's no name. It just says, 'I'm sorry' and 'I love you.'" She looked back at the bouquet. "And this makes no sense. Where's the lavender? This is a Mama Greenthumb's specialty. I send this to my mom every year for her Thanksgiving centerpiece. There's supposed to be lavender."

"Lavender?" Elandra asked, barely above a whisper.

"Yeah. It's Mama Greenthumb's signature flower. This makes no sense."

Elandra sighed, "It's Reid."

"What?"

"It's from Reid, hence the 'I'm sorry' and no lavender. He knows I can't stand lavender. It brings up bad memories." Elandra stared at the flowers, the strings on her heart pulling, but her mind kept it locked away.

Gen stood back and placed a hand on her hip. "Flowers? Getting the florist to remove their signature flower just because you don't like it? All right, El, now you have to tell me what happened with Kerith."

Elandra sighed, and knew she had to give in. "Okay." She placed the flowers down on the desk. "Well, you remember Mercedes mentioning the name Stephanie?" Her heart ached with the mere mention of the name.

"Yeah, but what does that have to do with you and Kerith? It's not his wife or something, is it?"

"No…" Elandra dragged out.

"El, who's Stephanie?"

"His fiancée." Elandra stared at Gen, who stood open-mouthed in shock. "Well, she would have been. She's his ex–fiancée."

"Ex-fiancée? Well that's okay, then. Who broke it off, him or her?"

"Actually, it wasn't so much broken off as…" Elandra drew a breath for strength. "She was murdered."

Gen's eyes opened wider than Elandra thought was humanly possible. "Oh, wow." Gen shook herself. "Didn't see that one coming." She looked up at Elandra in a moment of realization. "And from the way you had to ask about her, I'm guessing he didn't tell you about her."

"That about sums it up. But it's not the worst part, really, I mean not telling me is bad, believe me. But why she died is just as important. Remember how at the station he told us about his sister, Becky?"

Gen merely nodded.

"Well, remember they also said someone was trying to help her clean herself up? And that she was killed when Becky died?"

Gen could only nod again.

"Well that person who was helping Becky. That was Reid's fiancée."

Gen had to lean against the desk for support. "Holy shit."

Elandra's eyes darted to the ground in a hope that Gen wouldn't see the heartbreak and pain in them.

"Well, that certainly does change things, doesn't it?"

"Yeah. And to make it even worse—" Elandra was cut off.

"There's worse? It can't possibly get worse! Okay, wait, I need to sit down for this one." Gen pulled the chair over and sat, preparing herself for what Elandra had to say.

"The morning Becky and Stephanie were killed, Stephanie told Reid that she was pregnant."

Gen sat for a moment, her heart aching for Elandra. "Oh, honey…" she stood and embraced Elandra. "I'm so sorry, sweetie." She stood back and cupped Elandra's face. "But that was three years ago, honey, he's over her. He cares about you, that's all in the past."

"But he lied to me, he didn't tell me about her." Elandra looked at the flowers with deep sadness. *I told him my darkest secret but he didn't trust me enough to tell me his.* "Besides, he wants me to leave Hidden Desires. He says now I can get a real job, a respectable job."

"Respectable job? This is a respectable job, now I may be biased, but there is nothing wrong with the business." Gen replied.

"Well he figures that I don't need to work with the men anymore. I don't need them to look at me or touch me like a sex object anymore. He figures I can start a real life because I'd be with him. It's like he still thinks this is a whorehouse." Elandra's heart broke all over again.

*

"Come on, Kerith." Reilly wandered over to Kerith's desk and sat on the top. "You gotta take a break." He looked down at his friend with concern.

"Leave me alone, Reilly, I got work to do," Kerith muttered angrily and didn't look up from the papers.

"Yeah, but that's all you've been doing for two weeks." He tried to catch Kerith's eye, but when Kerith wouldn't respond, he ripped the papers out of his grasp.

"Hey!" Kerith's head jerked up.

"Look, it's for your own good."

"Well, some of us would like to help the public, you know, solve cases. Our job." Kerith grumbled, glaring at him.

"You've been throwing yourself into work for two weeks." He raised a hand to stop Kerith's objections. "And yeah I want to help, too, but you're taking it too far. You haven't taken a break since we arrested Mercedes."

"Well, that's 'cause some of us take our jobs seriously. Work doesn't stop just 'cause we made one arrest." Kerith snapped the papers back from Reilly.

"I'm not arguing that." He raised his hands up in surrender.

"Then what are you arguing? 'Cause we can't always afford to waste time."

"I'm arguing that you're driving yourself to a breaking point." His tone softened. "Look Kerith, as far as I can tell, it didn't go well with Elandra. I mean, I wouldn't expect it to, but it's been two weeks. Whatever happened can't be that big a deal anymore."

Kerith shifted his gaze away from Reilly. "You're right it didn't go well." He blew out a deep breath. "But she won't return my calls or anything." He stretched back in his chair. "And before you say anything, I did flowers, chocolates, the whole nine yards." He raked a hand through his hair. "And she still won't talk to me."

"So what? You're just giving up?" Reilly's tone lightened as he tried to cheer Kerith up.

"What else can I do? She doesn't want anything to do with me."

Reilly sat and considered it a minute. "Well, how about dinner? Yeah, you know like a peace offering."

"I don't know."

"No, it will work, trust me. It gets you two together, and you can talk through it. Chicks love when you do that. And since it's dinner, you can save yourself from saying something stupid by shoving food in your mouth." Reilly chuckled. "It's perfect. Come on, what do you have to lose? Worst case scenario she says no." Reilly sat there smiling, looking proud of himself.

"Well you're right about one thing: I've got nothing to lose." Kerith straightened up in his chair and reached for the phone. "It's worth a shot. But..." He gave a warning look to Reilly. "If she turns me down, then I throw myself into work, and you keep your opinions to yourself."

"Hell, it's worth a shot. God knows you're a pain to have around now." Reilly laughed as he rose and walked away.

Kerith took a deep breath and started to dial the phone.

Chapter 22

Kerith stood outside the door to Carmen's, the best Italian restaurant in town. He paced and checked his watch twenty times within two minutes. *Oh please, please let her show.* Kerith had invited Elandra to dinner, and through some coaxing from Gen no doubt, she had agreed to meet with him. Kerith continued to pace, worried that Elandra had changed her mind. *Please, please let her show.* He stopped in midstride as he spotted Elandra walking up the street toward him. His heart stopped, and he sighed in relief as she came within a few feet.

"I was worried you'd changed your mind." He placed his hands in his pockets and looked down at the ground sheepishly.

"I could never do that. I promised that I would meet you, and I don't go back on promises."

Kerith smiled.

"And besides, even if I did, I'd never have gotten away with it. Gen was there to push me out the door if need be."

Kerith's smile fell away, and he looked around nervously. "Uh, here, let me get the door for you." He reached forward and opened it.

They walked in and were met by the maitre d'. Kerith passed off his coat and surveyed the restaurant while the maitre d' helped Elandra take hers off with a shrug, revealing her slender shoulders. Kerith looked back at Elandra; she was in a deep emerald, satin, halter dress. The dress showed off her well-toned legs and slender arms, the top hugged her curves, and the bottom flowed out with regal elegance.

"Jesus Christ," Kerith swore under his breath and cleared his throat.

"You're table is ready, Mr. Reid. Right this way." The maitre d' led them into the restaurant.

The only table occupied was a with couple by the window, but the maitre d' placed them in the center of the room; under the domed ceiling that was painted with a midnight Italian sky, individual lights shining as each star. Within seconds of sitting down, a robust man walked up to the table, stretched his arms out in welcome, and smiled.

"And this would be Carmen," Kerith said by way of introduction.

"Ah, Mr. Reid, good to see you. And who is this beautiful flower?" the man said through a thick accent.

"This is Elandra, Carmen."

"You are very lucky, Mr. Reid, to have such a beautiful lady allow you to sit with her." He looked over at Elandra. "You let me know if you change your mind on this one." He motioned toward Kerith. "You let me know if you want to change to Italian. I got the best food; I feed you very well." Elandra smiled up at him, and he looked down at the tables. "Menus? No, no, no. This will not do. You let Carmen decide, I bring you best dish, okay?" He quickly snatched up the menus and disappeared into the kitchen.

Elandra and Kerith sat in silence until Carmen returned with two large bowls of pasta. "For Mr. Reid, the spaghetti Bolognese. And for the beautiful lady, tortellini with Alfredo sauce; the belly button of the goddess Venus for our very own Venus."

"Thank you, Carmen. There's no need to flirt with the lady. I'm pretty sure she has a date for this dinner already."

Elandra laughed at Kerith's obvious jealousy. "It looks wonderful, Carmen, almost too good to eat." She smiled up at him, earning a teasing glare from Kerith.

Carmen sighed, "Ah, you are my very own little Venus. But it appears that my welcome is wearing thin with Mr. Reid—so, enjoy your meal, my little Venus." And he left with a flourish.

"Now there's no need to encourage the man," Kerith laughed.

"Watch how you talk to me," Elandra said, getting the shocked reaction she was looking for from Kerith. "I am, after all, a goddess." She smiled teasingly.

"That you are," Kerith stated earnestly.

Elandra blushed and took to eating her pasta, and Kerith took that as his cue to dig in.

After some time, Kerith said, "I had every intention of telling about Stephanie." He watched Elandra's shoulders tense at the name. "But I…I just…I just believed that if I didn't talk about it, then it didn't happen. You know what I mean? That way it wasn't my fault."

Elandra looked up at him. "But it did happen." She sighed. "And it is a very important aspect of your life. It's a big part of what made you who you are." She placed her napkin across her bowl. "I just can't understand how you didn't trust me enough to tell me." She paused. "Even after I told you about being raped."

"No...oh, no, never think it was about trusting you. Never." He ran a hand through his hair. "It was never a matter of trusting you. Hell, I'd trust you with my life, and I can't even say that about some of the guys I work with at the station. It was never about trust, Elandra. I just...I didn't want..." He sighed with defeat. "You've been through so much in your life, things no one should ever have to go through. I guess I just didn't want to show you one more piece of evil in this world."

"You don't need to protect me, Reid." Elandra sat back and crossed her arms over her chest.

"You're right." Kerith sank back in his chair. Kerith sensed he was losing ground, and knew he had to make at least some headway. He dug around in his suit and pulled out a card. Kerith leaned across the table. "Here, this is a card for an advertising agent." He held up his hand to stop her objections. "Just work with him. I know you didn't plan on advertising, but a lot of guys could use your school. It could bring in a whole new clientele. And best of all..." He held his hand up in a flourish. "...no one will ever think Hidden Desires is a whorehouse again."

Elandra couldn't help but laugh. "Well, all right, I'll talk to him." She paused and turned serious. "But no promises, if I don't like what he has to say, then I'll look into someone else."

"He can help show that the school is the reputable institution that it is. You've worked so hard to build it, people should be able to see the love and care you put into it. He can help so that you have more free time to work with your clients, so you're not stuck doing paperwork all the time. Hidden Desires is a gem because of you. Just give it a chance—test the waters. That's all I'm asking for." He held his hands up in surrender.

Elandra knew they were no longer talking about the ad agent, and despite the fact that she was still apprehensive, her heart had decided that perhaps she could test the waters. "A chance sounds all right."

Kerith gave a small sigh of relief, knowing Elandra had read him right. "Well, then, what do you say to putting that chance in a safe spot for another day and me taking you home?"

Elandra nodded her consent, and they left the restaurant with a little more hope and a little more comfort in each other.

Chapter 23

Kerith jogged down the steps of Elandra's house, feeling more confident about their relationship. He started whistling to himself, and he felt himself smiling for the first time in weeks. Kerith sauntered down the sidewalk toward his car, feeling like everything was finally going his way. Just as he was placing his keys in the door, his eyes were attracted to a puff of smoke from under the streetlamp across from him. Kerith glanced up just in time to see the stranger emerge from the darkness of the dead lamp and into the brightness of the others. Kerith felt his body tense, sensing that something wasn't quite right. The light hit just behind the figure, making it impossible for Kerith to see his face.

"You know you shouldn't waste your time," the shadow said.

"Excuse me?" Kerith asked defensively.

"She'll never want you. You're not good enough for her," the shadow replied, confident in his answers.

"And who would the she be?" Kerith's police instincts were kicking in, forcing the stranger to say exactly what he meant.

"Cassidy, of course." The shadow took a long drag of his cigarette.

"Cassidy?" Kerith jogged his memory and everything clicked into place. "Oh, you mean Elandra. That's her name now, and I've got a pretty good idea that she's got you to thank for the change." His hand dropped to his side.

"You don't deserve her."

"And you do?" Kerith leaned forward, onto the roof of his car.

"You'd do best to stay away from her," the shadow threatened.

"Oh yeah? Or else what? You'll blow smoke in my face?" Kerith laughed, "She can decide who she wants herself."

"She *belongs* to me," the shadow stated in all seriousness.

"Belongs? I'm sorry you're in the wrong era, buddy. Cassidy, as you call her, is not an item to be bought or won." Kerith stepped from around his car, trying to maneuver the shadow into the light.

"Well, we have a history—one that a pretty boy like you, could never come in between. So don't waste your time."

"Well, it's nice you think I'm pretty, but you're not my type."

"Shut up!" the shadow shouted at him. "I've had enough of your wise-ass remarks. You stay away from her! Believe me, you don't want to play with this fire—you may get burned." He threw his cigarette on the ground and stamped it out with his foot, crushing it into the pavement as he turned as if to leave.

Dammit, Kerith thought, *you can't just walk away. Come on, try to take a piece out of me.* "Is that so? Well that will be a bit of a problem, now won't it?" *Come on...* "I mean, the real issue is whether she can stay away from me. I have no trouble saying our time together is explosive." Kerith smirked. *Come on! Come at me, you jackass.* "She's just so hot when we're together. It's like we could set the place on fire just by having sex." *Just one hit, that's all I need. Come on!*

The shadow stopped dead in its tracks and spun on its heel. "What did you say?" he hissed.

Kerith smirked, feeling triumphant. *That's it, come on...* "I said Elandra and I have the most explosive sex."

"You asshole! How dare you touch her!" the shadow screamed and ran at Kerith.

Kerith didn't have enough time to react. He fell to the ground underneath the weight of the shadow. They struggled back and forth, throwing punches here and blocking others there. Profanity marked every movement, and soon blood trickled in response. Kerith kicked the shadow off him and jumped up. But before he knew what was happening, the shadow kicked his feet out from under him, and he fell flat on his back, the shadow looming over him.

Kerith stared up at the figure above. "So what? Now you kill me?"

"No. She wouldn't want that." The shadow turned and started to walk away. "But stay away from her, or else I won't be responsible for my actions." He called over his shoulder, "I mean it, stay away from her. I'll know if you don't."

Kerith rubbed at his bloody lip. "Let me guess, 'cause you're the Shadow? And the Shadow knows." Kerith laughed and looked up into the blackness. "Hey!" he called into the now empty night.

Chapter 24

He scrubbed furiously at his hands, trying to rub his rage out. He rubbed until his hands became red and raw, and then he threw the brush into the sink with such force that it broke in two. He placed both hands on either side of the sink and stared up into the mirror. He turned his head this way and that, looking at the small scratches and bruises that would appear later. He tilted his head to the right and examined his eye. There was a cut just above his left eye, and it was causing blood to trickle down and into his vision.

He yanked a small towel off the rack beside the sink and made to dab at his forehead. He blew out a breath, preparing himself. He touched the cloth to his face and winced at the feel of the rough cloth against his smooth skin. He wiped away the blood, placed the towel on the edge of the sink, and examined his cut again. *Bastard's lucky I won't need stitches. It's gonna leave one hell of a scar though.*

He looked in the mirror, and his mind took over. As he stared into his reflection, it morphed and turned into images. Elandra, he had called her Elandra. *But she still is and will always be my Cassidy.*

The images became that of his Cassidy stretched out on a bed beneath someone. He couldn't tell who; he could only see their back. He watched as she withered, moaned, and arched. The images in the mirror sharpened and zoomed in on Cassidy's face. He watched as her face transformed into one belonging to intense passion and desire. He watched her face as she climaxed and rode out a wave of ecstasy as the man above her arched in his climax and then fall in peace on top of her. The images then transformed as he watched the man above her roll to the side.

His own face twisted in anger as the face of the man with Cassidy became clear. He watched as that face grinned up at him, smug and taunting. It was the detective—that pompous ass who had left him cut. His rage grew as his eyes bore into the face in the mirror. Finally his anger boiled over, and he drove his fist into the mirror with a crash. Pieces of the mirror fell into the sink and crashed to the tiled floor of the bathroom. He stared at his broken face in the pieces that remained in the frame, and he looked down into the sink at the fallen parts, but the images played on. Every piece, every crack held the detective's face. Smiling at him. Laughing at him. Taunting him.

He stormed out of the bathroom and into the greater, sparse room. He would make the detective pay. He would make him pay for touching her. For...for...he couldn't bring himself to even think the words. The detective had touched his precious Cassidy, and for that he would pay. He walked through the room over to his sorry excuse for a kitchen. His brother had really let him down on this one; there had been much better places, but his brother had insisted on this one. And as always, Jacob had listened to his wiser brother. But soon, soon it would all be better. He would have his Cassidy, and that detective would be out of their lives forever. He pulled open a drawer and rummaged through the mess. He picked up what he'd been looking for and headed toward the door.

He opened the door and looked back into the empty room, speaking to it. "I told you not to play with fire," he laughed. "Now you're going to get burned." He closed the door behind him and headed off into the night.

*

Kerith opened the door, tossed his keys on the inside table, and slid the door closed with his back. He leaned up against it a moment, trying to think through the events of the night. He ran a hand over his exasperated face and winced as he touched his lip. *Right, gotta clean that up.* He walked down the hall to his bathroom, rolling his now-sore shoulders as he went. He entered his bathroom and immediately started rifling through the closet. Whoever had decided to put a closet in the bathroom was a genius. He pushed things around, looking for antiseptic, shoving towels around and dropping razor blades, deodorant, and aftershave onto the floor.

"Well, dammit," he swore as he bent down to pick everything up. "I'm not that bad. You don't have to be suicidal and jump for it," he swore at everything. "Aw, Christ, I'm talking to objects." He laughed at himself as he grabbed the bottle he was looking for and some cotton balls. He turned around to the sink, looking in the mirror. "I gotta admit, he may be a psychotic jackass, but he sure can hit." He lifted his head up, examining his lip. He soaked a cotton ball in liquid and gingerly dabbed at the cut. "Jesus Christ," he swore as he cleansed it.

He tried cleaning it a couple seconds more, but he couldn't take the pain, so he just threw the cotton away and left everything on the sink as he went out into his living room. He walked across the room to his makeshift office and clicked on his computer. As it started booting up, he walked back across to his kitchen. He made coffee, trying to let the aroma trigger his senses. *I've got to find this guy—but how? Where?*

He grabbed his now-hot cup of java. "See, now this is coffee. None of that whipped, seasoned crap; just coffee," he mused to himself as he passed back through the room and sat in front of his computer.

He stared at the screen before him, wondering what to do next. He sipped at his coffee and let his mind wander. He stretched back in his chair and thought out loud, hoping something would click.

"All right what do we know?" He took another sip, wincing as the hot liquid touched his cut lip. "He likes to burn girls; old-school thought, saying she belongs to him; hits like a brick wall…" He rubbed his jaw back and forth. "And…" His feet hit the floor with his next thought. "The senator! She said he looked exactly like the senator!"

He leaned forward to the computer and grabbed the phone beside him as he went. He started typing furiously as he dialed a familiar number and hugged the phone between his shoulder and chin. He pulled up search engines and listened as the phone continued to ring at the other end.

Finally it kicked over to a machine. "Dammit, Reilly, you're supposed to be home. Well, if I'm interrupting something, it better damn well be sex, 'cause dammit, man, this is important." He juggled the phone and took it in hand again. "I need everything you can find on Senator Victor Prescott. Yes, you're hearing me right: Senator Victor Prescott. I can't explain now, but I want as much info as you can get, and I want it yesterday. You got me? I want it all. Hell, I'll take his fifth-grade report card if you can find it. I just want everything anyone has on him. Call me when you get it, and Reilly, get it fast!" He hung up and focused back on the computer.

He stared at his search results and ran a hand through his hair. "One thousand, five hundred and seventy-two. Jesus Christ, it's going to be a long night." He looked over at his now-empty coffee cup and headed back to the kitchen before falling back into the chair, preparing himself for the night ahead.

*

Elandra sat on the floor of her bedroom with small photo boxes all around her. She shuffled through the pictures and mementos, trying to piece together how she felt. Each box held a part of her life; a part that included someone else. One held tickets to the Santana concert she had gone to with Bradley. Another all the movie stubs she had had to pay for herself from her time with Malcolm. Yet another box even held the attempt at a love-song mix created by the kindhearted Daniel. Elandra smiled at the memories and remembered that, with each relationship, there had been good times. She pulled out pictures of each of the men from her life. She flipped through them, laughing at fond memories and making faces at others.

She drew a deep breath as she pulled a dusty box toward her and carefully lifted the lid. Elandra felt her chest tighten as she stared down at the contents. She picked up a faded picture and held it close to her, examining the faces and feeling her eyes start to fill with tears. She wiped them away with her hand as she continued to look down at her family. She ran her fingers over the picture, believing that she could be closer to them just by touching it. She placed the photo back in the box and continued to look at the memories of the life she'd had to leave behind. She pulled out old class photos and drawings she had done as a tot and picked up a small, stuffed dog. She hugged it to her chest and let its scent surround her. It had once smelled like home, and every once in a while, if she concentrated really hard, she could catch the faintest whiff. She held it away from her and smiled down at it. "We've been through some really tough times, you and me." Elandra's mind played through all the times she had sought comfort in this little creature. When she broke her arm when she was five; when her grandmother died when she was eight; the first time she was dumped; when she failed a test. And again the night she was raped, and many nights after. "You're the only one I have left," she sniffed. "The only one I didn't leave behind." She gulped back some tears and gently placed it back in the box. She then took a deep breath and removed her birth certificate. She stared at it, and this time, let the tears fall as she read the name imprinted on it: Cassidy Grace Montgomery. Elandra wiped at her eyes, feeling her heart break as she remembered everything she had had to give up. She placed the lid gingerly back on the box as she tried to sniff away her memories, and she pushed the box off to the side.

Elandra heaved a great sigh and shook off the painful memories. She looked around her room and silently scolded herself for getting caught up in the past. *I'm alive. I'm alive, and I have my work, and better yet, my friends. I may not have everything I want, but…but I have time—I have all the time in the world. I could…I could travel. I could…write instruction manuals for men.* She smiled. *I could teach them to cherish. To love. To share.* Elandra emitted a disbelieving snort, she threw her hand to her face and looked around to make sure no one heard. *Reid could use that lesson—sharing.* She had shared her darkest secret with him, and he couldn't return it. *Why are men so difficult?* She heaved a frustrated sigh, but realized that it was men. It wasn't just Reid. *All men have problems sharing. All men have trouble letting the women they care about in, letting us see their flaws. They think they're protecting us; they think they're doing what's best. And trying to spare the woman you love pain is charming, admirable even. They try so hard, but then they go too far. Leave Hidden Desires because he can look after me. I can get a respectable job.* She snorted, *he did find me an ad agent. He said I could focus on my clients. I guess no man would really want his wife turning on every man she works with. That is what my school is for, though, to turn people on. He did talk about building my business though. Maybe…maybe Reid…Maybe he deserves another chance—a chance to make things right.* Elandra took a deep breath, trying to sort through her thoughts. She checked herself. *Time, I need time. I may have all the time in the world, but there's no need to make rash decisions. I have time. I don't want to lose time by acting too quick. I don't want to lose anymore than I already have.*

Elandra carefully went through every other box and finally came upon the plastic gum-machine ring that Malcolm had given her. He had never even bought her real jewelry, and they'd had a discussion about engagement rings. Elandra remembered when Malcolm explained his thoughts behind the rings: since the bride was the only one to wear it, Malcolm saw no reason for the groom to purchase it. He had actually believed and had even told her that, since the groom got nothing out of it, he saw no reason for a man to spend all that money on jewelry he wouldn't even get to own. Elandra laughed as she looked at the ring, remembering his stoic expression as he had told her his views. That had been the breaking point of their relationship; not that it had been that big of a loss. A plastic ring—a plastic engagement ring…

Elandra sighed as she placed the ring back in the box. "I bet Stephanie got a real ring." She glared at the ring in the box and slapped the lid on. "He couldn't even tell me he had been engaged." She felt her irritation grow and the pain rising back up in her chest.

She closed and gathered up all the boxes, feeling no more in control of her emotions and just as confused as when she had started. She climbed into bed and let her sleepy mind contemplate the one question she couldn't answer: *Does Reid deserve another chance?*

Chapter 25

As Kerith stirred, in the haze of his head he heard the shrill of the phone from somewhere in his apartment. He grabbed a pillow and shoved it over his head, trying to drown out the sound, but it wouldn't cease. He moved sluggishly and stretched, trying to clear his mind of sleep. He stretched across the bed, and his hand slid under a pillow and hit something hard.

"What the..." he muttered in among a yawn. He pulled his arm back to reveal the phone, which rang like a siren now near his head. "Fuck..." He twisted the phone upright and pressed *talk*. "Yeah?"

"I get a loud phone message in the middle of really hot sex telling me to look up the senator, and now you're asleep? Life's not fair," the voice groaned.

"Reilly?" Kerith continued to stretch and yawn, finally shaking off the last of his sleep fog.

"Yeah. I mean, you could have just left a nice message. Fucking scared the shit out of Melanie." He grumbled,

"You couldn't have just left a nice message or waited until morning…"

"I mess up your night?" Kerith chuckled, "No worries, man, you'll get a new girl tonight, and it will be like it never happened."

"Oh, ha-ha, Reid. You know, some of us don't just go and sleep with our suspects, like you."

"Hey, hey. Low blow." He raised his hands in surrender even though Reilly couldn't see him. "So you got anything for me or not?"

"Well yeah, good morning to you, too, sunshine." Reilly's tone took on a bite.

"Sorry, man, I was up 'til four-thirty this morning trying to find something, anything on the senator." Kerith continued to stretch in bed. "Did you know he was on his high school's track team?"

"Yeah, great, whatever. Look, I don't know what you were looking for or what you wanted, but I came up with the usual: no parking tickets, one speeding ticket—you know, normal stuff. I mean I can…"

Kerith cut him off, sniffing the air. "What the hell is that?"

"What?" Reilly asked confused.

"Something doesn't smell right." Kerith rose from the bed.

"You try to cook something last night?" Reilly laughed.

"Ha-ha. I'm actually a very good cook." Kerith walked over to the closed door and froze. "Holy shit!" he yelled.

"Dammit, Reid." Reilly cleared out his ear. "What the hell is going on?"

"Call the fire department, Reilly!" Kerith yelled into the phone as he raced back toward the bed and grabbed a pillow, ripping the case off and covering his hand with it.

"Fire department? What the hell is going on, Reid?" Reilly yelled back into the phone.

"My fucking place is on fire!" Kerith yelled, moving back toward to door. "There's smoke coming from under the door. Shit, shit!" He reached forward with his covered hand and tentatively reached for the knob. "Jesus Christ!" he swore as he jerked the door open and jumped out into the hall.

"Okay, just stay calm, Reid, I'll call the fire department. You just…you get out, and I'll be there to help as soon as I can." Kerith could hear Reilly rushing around through the phone.

Kerith looked down the hall toward his own bedroom; he had apparently crashed in the spare bedroom. He could see the flames lick at the door frame and walls.

"Jesus Christ!" he swore again.

"Reid! Reid! Get the hell out of there, okay? Get the hell out of your apartment!" Reilly ordered into the phone.

"Right, right."

"I'll call the fire department." Reilly hung up without even saying good-bye.

Kerith ran out to his living room and froze in horror. His office was up in flames, and they were working their way toward him. He ran to his front door and pulled the fire alarm.

He bolted out into the hallway and started yelling down the hall, "Fire! Fire! Everybody get the hell out!"

Kerith kept yelling until he started seeing faces appearing in the hall, wondering what he was screaming about. "Fire! Get the hell out! Get everyone out!" He watched as people disappeared back into their apartments, and others raced toward the stairs. He flew across the hall to his next-door neighbor's and started pounding at the door. "Mr. Carson! Mr. Carson!" he yelled at the door.

The door creaked open. "What's going on, Kerith?" asked the elderly man.

"Mr. Carson, the building's on fire. Come on, we gotta get you outta here." The words tumbled out of his mouth.

"Oh…oh…" the elderly man clutched at his chest.

"It's okay, Mr. Carson, I'll get you outta here, don't worry. Come on, deep breaths, Mister Carson. I can't have you having a heart attack on me." Kerith reached into the apartment and steadied the man.

The man slowed his breathing and shook himself, coughing. "Okay." He hacked, "Okay. I'm all right now."

Kerith ushered him out the door and held his arm, guiding him down the hallway.

The man suddenly stopped and yelled, trying to turn around. "Gloria! I can't leave Gloria!"

"I'll get her." Kerith glanced around the hall and grabbed his other neighbor. "Mrs. Cortez, can you help Mr. Carson out? I gotta get Gloria."

"Yes, yes, of course." The woman took the elderly man's arm and kept heading toward the stairs.

"Be careful!" the man shouted over his shoulder, coughing in the process.

Kerith turned and ran back down the hall. He flew into his neighbor's apartment. He rushed around the room, searching every surface. His eyes finally fell on the top of an old TV, and he raced over.

Kerith picked up an elegant picture frame. "Don't worry, Gloria, I wasn't about to leave you." Kerith spoke to the picture and suddenly froze.

He bolted back across the hall to his own apartment and flew into his living room, jumping back just in time to miss some flames leaping out at him. He ducked and grabbed something off his coffee table and jerked out of the way. He sped back out into the hall and down toward the stairs. He took the stairs two at a time and bounded out into the open, fresh air. He fell into the street and hurried over to the gathering crowd.

He searched the faces and found Mr. Carson. "Here you go, Mr. Carson." He handed the frame over.

Mr. Carson took the frame in his fragile hands. "Perfect as ever," he coughed. "See, I told you he was a good boy, Gloria," he said to the picture and smiled up at Kerith. "Thank you. I…I don't know what I would do without her." He coughed, and tears pricked at his eyes.

Kerith smiled down at him. "Don't mention it. Couldn't leave a gorgeous girl like that in danger." Kerith turned and faced the crowd, addressing them. "I'm sorry to have woken you all, but I woke up, and my apartment was on fire. Now, all your homes may not be at risk, but being such a small building I didn't want to chance anything. Is everyone out and okay?"

"Yeah," came the response from the crowd.

Kerith turned back, raked a hand through his hair, and sighed. He watched the flames reflected in the windows, and his whole world fell into a dreamlike haze. He continued to stare up at the apartment until the fire crew came, and he was only brought back to reality when Reilly placed a hand on his shoulder.

"Reid."

Kerith turned to face him.

"Jesus, Reid. What the hell happened?"

"Fire…" Kerith's voice sounded distant, even to him. "I had a fire…"

"Yeah, I see, but what started it?"

Everything suddenly clicked into place. "Elandra."

"Elandra started it?" Reilly asked, confused.

"No. No." His eyes cleared. "Shit, Reilly, Elandra's in trouble, come on."

"What? What's going on?" Reilly stood, rooted to the ground.

"I'll explain on the way. I gotta borrow your car." They turned and ran down the street, Kerith leaving his apartment behind him, still burning bright.

Chapter 26

Elandra shuffled papers at the front desk and then ran through the calendar once more.

"El, honey, you've been bustling around here all morning," Gen said as she walked up, "But you haven't done a thing. It's like you're shifting papers just for the sake of it."

"I'm organizing." Elandra looked at her defiantly.

"Sweetie, you're more in the way than anything." Gen looked at her pointedly.

Elandra sighed, "I know. I just don't know what to do with myself." Her shoulders fell.

"Go to him," Gen stated as if it were clear as day.

"If you mean Reid, well, just forget it," she huffed, "He lied to me, remember?"

"He didn't lie. He just didn't tell you about Stephanie."

"You mean his dead fiancée."

"Look, honey, can you imagine how hard it must have been for him to tell you? Don't you have some secret that it would hurt to tell, let alone think about?"

Elandra's mind raced back to the café where she told Kerith her secret about being raped. Elandra remembered how hard it had been to talk about, but also how supportive Kerith had been and how important she had felt it was to tell him. Elandra's heart gave way a little, but she still felt unsure. Elandra looked up at Gen, her eyes betraying her conflicting emotions.

"Look, I'm not saying just forgive and forget," Gen added, "but at least understand how hard it probably was." She placed a hand on Elandra's shoulder in support.

"I know." Elandra placed her hand over Gen's and looked into Gen's challenging eyes. "I do." She chuckled at Gen raised eyebrow. "I do understand." She sighed, "It's just hard to accept that he was engaged to another woman."

Gen looked at her with compassion. "I know, sweetie, but you can't live in her shadow. He obviously loves you, and you should let him. You're the one who controls whether it's her or you."

Elandra smiled up at her. "You're right." Elandra raked a hand through her hair, silently laughing to herself that she had started to take on his quirks. "But what about leaving the school?"

"But you said that at dinner he gave you info for an ad agent and that it could help you focus on lessons. Look, he wouldn't have searched out a guy if he still thought we were a whorehouse. He wants to help you and Hidden Desires. If you ask me not only does he understand but he fully supports you and the school."

Elandra directed a mock glare at Gen, "You're right

"Of course I'm right." Gen smiled. "I learned everything I know from you."

Elandra laughed, "Thanks, hon." She added as Gen left the room.

Elandra turned back to the desk and placed her hand on the phone. *Come on, it had to be just as hard to tell me about Stephanie as it was for me to tell him about being raped.* While Elandra's gut was still weary, her heart had decided that it belonged to him. Elandra smiled as she raised the receiver to her ear. Elandra's fingers had merely brushed the keypad when the front door burst open.

"Reid?" Elandra stood open-mouthed in shock.

"Grab your stuff, we gotta go," his words spilled out.

Elandra placed the receiver back in its cradle. "What are you talking about? What's going on?"

Kerith raced behind the counter, "No time to explain now. We gotta go." He grabbed her hand and started to drag her up the stairs.

Elandra hurried along behind him, "What's going on? And why are you covered in dirt?" she asked, finally taking in his disheveled appearance.

He pulled her down the hall, opening the first door he saw. "Someone set fire to my place." He turned abruptly, leaving Gen confused and standing in the open doorway. "Where the hell is your bedroom?"

"What's going on?" Gen called after them.

Elandra glanced back at Gen with a lost look on her face as she continued to follow Kerith down the hall.

She turned back to face him. "What happened? Is everything at your place okay?"

Kerith kept throwing doors open along the way and pulled her up the next flight of stairs. They finally came to the end of the hall and faced three doors, one on either side and one in front.

"Which one?" Kerith demanded.

"The one on the left is a storage closet, the one on the right is the attic, and the one in front is my bedroom."

Kerith threw the center door open and rushed in, letting go of her hand. "You grab a bag and your toiletries; I'll grab your clothes." He raced toward the dresser and started opening drawers, throwing handfuls of clothes on the bed.

Elandra stood still and crossed her arms over her chest, "Reid…" Elandra grew impatient when Kerith merely kept throwing clothes.

"Get moving, sugar. We have to get you out of here," he ordered without even pausing as he moved to her closet and continued his work.

"Reid!" Elandra yelled, halting his movements so he looked over at her. "What the hell is going on? Don't give me orders! What happened to you?" She huffed, "And like I told you before: This is my home." She walked over to the bed. "I'm not going anywhere." She sat down resolutely.

Kerith walked over to the bed, shifted some clothes, and sat down. "Okay." He drew a deep breath. "After I dropped you off from dinner last night, some guy came up and told me to stay away from you. And I'm guessing it was that crazy stalker guy of yours, 'cause when I woke up this morning, my place was on fire."

Elandra leaned forward. "Oh, Reid…"

"I was told I'm lucky I woke up when I did, 'cause otherwise I'd be burnt to a crisp like the rest of my apartment. And I got Reilly to thank for waking me up."

Elandra placed a hand on his knee. "I'm so sorry."

Kerith felt Elandra's concern and tenderness wrap around him like a warm blanket. "It's just stuff, it's no big deal." He sighed, "But either way, I got a feeling that when he finds out I'm not fried chicken, he'll come after you."

Elandra gasped as everything sunk in. "You really think so?"

Kerith nodded his head solemnly. "Yeah, I do. Which is why Reilly and me talked to the feds and arranged for you to stay in a nearby safe house. We just gotta grab your stuff. But it's best if we go as soon as possible."

Elandra's mind and body flew into a blind panic. She jumped up off the bed and raced toward the bathroom. "You're right. There's a bag at the bottom of the closet. Just throw everything in, and I'll grab the stuff from here."

∗

They worked fast, clothes and movements flying around the room. They only stopped long enough to fill Gen in. Elandra and Gen stopped at the front door as Kerith ran out to the car.

"You'll be able to handle everything?" Elandra asked, concerned.

Gen handed her a small suitcase. "Yes, now go."

"You'll look after everything?"

"Of course I will, El. Now go." Gen shooed her down the steps. "It's not safe for you out in the open like this."

Elandra raced down the steps and into the waiting car. As Kerith pulled away, Elandra stared back at the house. *This is the second time he's running me out of my own home.* Elandra watched until the house was out of sight. Fear gripped her body, but it was her broken heart over having to flee her home that ripped at her soul.

Chapter 27

Elandra swallowed her fear as she looked around the room. *Kerith had been threatened.* She wandered the room, touching every surface and feeling the smoothness of it all melt away from her fingertips. *Reid's life has been threatened and it's all because of me!* She walked to the window and stared out at the water. She opened the window and let the breeze wash over her as it swirled in the room. She breathed in the smell of fresh cut grass and longed to be out in the sun. The breeze seemed to momentarily remove the rest of the world. It made her feel free of all the problems that waited for her back home. She watched the water ripple in the wind and wondered if this was why people took to the water; why people would spend thousands on boats, only to use them a few times a year. Elandra took a moment to enjoy the feeling of freedom, and let herself feel like who she used to be. She drew one last deep breath, closed the window, and heaved a great sigh, remembering why she was here. This building had once been someone's home; this had been someone's bedroom. *Reid's lost his home because of me.* Elandra realized that she had almost forgotten what a real home felt like. She had been working so hard and living at the school. Elandra drifted away into her own thoughts. *Reid's lost his home because of me. I've put the whole school in danger. Chloe...Chloe's gone because of me.* Elandra's thoughts were disjointed and jumbled, causing her to become so lost that she never even heard the door open.

Kerith slipped into the room and quietly closed the door behind him. He stood and stared at her for a moment. She looked so peaceful. A smile crept onto his face. She reminded him of home, and it had been so long since he had seen it. He walked up behind her.

She felt his hands slide along her sides, and she closed her eyes, fading into her memories. It wasn't until he started to kiss the back of her neck that she crashed back to reality. She stepped out of his arms, feeling torn. *He's in trouble, because of me. I can't handle this on my own. He's lost everything because of me. But I want him to protect me. His life has been threatened. I've put him in danger. I can't let him get hurt because of me.*

Elandra drew in a deep breath, looking up into Kerith's expecting eyes. "You don't smell like smoke anymore."

Kerith chuckled, running a hand through his hair. "Yeah, it was the first chance I got to have a shower since my apartment."

He looked over at Elandra, feeling his tension melt away. His eyes drank in her appearance; she wore simple jeans, a white T-shirt, and a light brown, wool, hooded sweater. Her hair was pulled back in a half-ponytail, and on anyone else he would merely have skimmed over these details. But on Elandra, with her hands in her back pockets, in an entirely nervous stance—there was just something about her. She couldn't have looked more innocent, but somehow still managed to look like sin incarnate. Kerith knew she must be frightened and that this was a difficult time, but he still felt himself responding simply to being in the same room with her. He simply had to look at her and he felt his love for her. Kerith recognized, then and there, that he was never going to let any harm come to her.

"I made sure the firefighters had everything under control, organized everything, and then I came straight for you," he said, smiling over at her.

"Why did you bring me here?" Elandra knew the pain she felt was reflected in her eyes.

"I brought you here to protect you," Kerith replied, feeling the answer was obvious.

"But why?"

Kerith's mind was lost in confusion, and he didn't like where Elandra seemed to be leading them. "You're originally from Ireland, aren't you?" he asked, trying to distract her.

Elandra sighed, "Yes, my family came here when I was five years old. But why does that matter?"

"Becky and I had to leave Ireland when I was sixteen and she was thirteen. But I've always intended to go back."

Her tension eased a little, as she could sense his pain. "That's so sad."

"Our mom had been a housekeeper to a wealthy family, and she had an affair with the husband. Becky and I were his bastard children." He paused, trying to swallow back his pain and show Elandra he trusted her. "But when he died, his wife threw us all out. I was fifteen at that point, and when my mother got sick, we went to the wife for help, but she refused. Then, when my mother died, we went to try to work for the family. But she thought Becky and I were trying to extort money from them, so she drove us from Ireland. I brought Becky here, thinking that, if we could make a life, then we could go back. I wanted to prove myself to her, because…because…" He stumbled over his words.

Elandra came up and placed her arms around him, trying to hug away his pain. "You don't have to prove anything to that woman."

Kerith removed himself from her embrace, instantly missing her touch. He shook his head. "No, I do. You see," he sighed, "she has my half-brother. He has autism and needs special care and attention. I was a real big brother to him until we were kicked out. He's a year younger than Becky. And because of his condition, he didn't have many friends growing up, but he was my best friend."

Elandra felt her heart ache for him. She had the strongest urge to comfort him, but she was still weary. *He has experienced so much pain in his life. I can't add to it. I can't let him be hurt because of me.* She felt her heart rip itself in half. *I can't be with him. I can't put him in danger and if we were together. I love him too much to let him get hurt over me. He's experienced so much pain already.*

Kerith wandered over and looked out the window. "After Stephanie was murdered, there was a while when my desire to go home was the only thing that kept me going—the chance to see Clayton again." He turned to face her again. "That's where I got the name. My brother's name is Clayton." He smiled, lost in his own thoughts.

Elandra's heart fell. *He's a fighter. He's fought so hard to try to make things right. He'll never simply let me go, he'll fight for me. But I can't let him, I can't let him get hurt. So much trouble, so much danger since he met me.* Elandra's mind flashed and she latched onto the idea.

"You know, I've been in nothing but trouble and danger since I met you." She crossed her arms over her chest, trying to look angry. She took in his confused look and knew she'd have to just dive right into this plan. "I don't think we should be together. Bad things just keep happening when we are, I...I just don't think I can deal with anymore danger because of you." She thrust her chin out in defiance.

If Kerith was going to respond, it was lost when a loud crash came from down in the kitchen.

Chapter 28

Kerith pulled out his gun and quietly headed toward the stairs, Elandra following close behind him. They crept down the stairs, as silent as could be. When they reached the bottom, Kerith peered around the corner. Elandra stepped out into the open to see. Kerith caught sight of her out of the corner of his eye and felt a sudden urge to protect her. His arm shot out across her chest and pressed her back against the wall. Elandra gasped in response to his touch and gazed down at his arm, which was casually splayed across her breasts. Kerith looked at her with compassion and let his eyes drop down to his outstretched arm. He blushed at its precarious position, and Elandra had to stifle a laugh. *He's done so much more with me, but this he blushes at.*

"Stay here," Kerith mouthed to her, being careful not to make a sound.

He crept forward, clinging to the walls as he carefully made his way down the hall to the kitchen. Gun poised, Kerith slowed his pace as he neared the source of the noise. He inched forward, glancing into the little bit of the kitchen he could see from his hiding place. His eyes swept the visible floor of the kitchen and stopped cold when he saw Reilly lying on the floor. Kerith could only make out Reilly's head, eyes closed, face-down on the floor.

"Shit," he swore under his breath.

"Is he okay?" a whisper came from beside him.

Kerith jumped at the unexpected sound, "What the fuck?" he said in a crystal-clear voice. His head jerked to the side and looked down at Elandra. "I told you to stay there." He hissed out in a whisper.

"I wasn't about to stay put. I'm not some damsel in distress, Reid." She glared at him.

"Oh, for Pete's sake," he groaned.

They stared at each other for a few moments, battling for control—but then Kerith caught a reflection in Elandra's eye. He stilled himself long enough to watch Elandra's eyes grow wide before he swung around. His arm whipped back, but he didn't make contact. Kerith suddenly doubled over as he felt the burning pain of a fist making contact with his stomach.

He staggered into the kitchen and threw his arm back behind him. "Stay back, Elandra!" he wheezed.

Elandra pressed her back flat against the wall and watched in terror from the hallway. Kerith swung blindly and felt the impact of a fist hit his face, pushing him to the side. As Kerith's head was turned, the intruder charged low at him and contacted with Kerith's midsection, pushing him back into the counter. Kerith shoved the intruder off and swung. He made contact with the man's face and watched as blood spattered across the air. Kerith raised his gun in an attempt to knock the intruder unconscious, but the man had other ideas. He easily knocked Kerith's hand to the side and punched him once more in the stomach. He twisted Kerith's hand backward, sending the gun crashing to the floor. But before the man had time to reach it, Kerith kicked the wayward gun to the other side of the room. Kerith and the man wrestled some more, fighting for control. Kerith was able to lock the intruder's arms back and reach to his own left leg. He pulled up his pant leg, and in one swift movement, removed his spare gun from its holder. Kerith lifted his right knee up and shoved it into the intruder's stomach, causing him to fall backward, his backside hitting the floor with a hard thump. Both men raggedly drew in their breath as Kerith raised the new gun and leveled it at the intruder.

"It's okay, Elandra, you can come out now," Kerith said between wheezing breaths.

The intruder raised himself up and leaned against the counter across from Kerith, using the back of his hand to wipe away some blood from his mouth. Kerith and the man stared at each other as Elandra ran over to Reilly's body. She bent over him and felt for a pulse.

"He's unconscious, but still alive," she said, looking up. "But, Reid, he's only just alive. He needs help."

Kerith kept his eyes trained on the intruder. He tossed his cell phone over to Elandra. "Here, call for backup and an ambulance."

Elandra caught the phone in one swift move and started furiously dialing the numbers. She lost herself in getting help, disregarding the two men in front of her.

"How's your place, detective?" the intruder chuckled. "Find it a little hot this morning?"

"Actually, it felt like a nice day at the beach," Kerith chimed, watching the intruder's eyes flicker with anger in response.

The intruder cleared his throat, trying to regain his composure. "Well, it's a good thing you didn't get a burn then." He looked over at Elandra, who was still lost in a phone conversation. "You should have given up when I gave you the chance."

"Actually, considering your position now, it looks like you're the one who should have given up when I gave *you* the chance," Kerith replied, feeling in control.

The intruder chuckled, but he never tore his gaze away from Elandra. "You're not good enough for her. You never will be."

"I think she's able to make that decision on her own."

"You don't get it." The intruder finally raised his eyes to meet Kerith's. "She and I belong together. She is mine and mine alone." His eyes travelled back to Elandra. "Not even you can stop us from being together."

Kerith's eyes followed the man's back to Elandra, and before Kerith had time to react, the intruder stepped forward and swung his body around so that his back was to Kerith. In one fluid movement, he twisted the arm that held the gun and shot Kerith in the leg. As he started to fall, the intruder raised the gun back up and hit it hard against Kerith's head. Kerith was unconscious before he hit the floor. The man quickly stepped across Reilly's body and was upon Elandra. The last thing she saw was a white cloth heading toward her face.

Chapter 29

landra rolled her head and started to wake. She tried to move her arms, but found they were stuck to her sides. She slowly opened her eyes and took in her surroundings. She was in a bleak apartment. To her left was a dilapidated kitchen with a lone table near the wall; and there was a sorry excuse for a bathroom by what had to be the front door. Elandra twisted in her spot, trying to get a better look at the room, and she finally looked down at herself. *I'm tied to a chair!* Elandra's mind raced in a blind panic. *Oh, God! What happened to me?* Elandra felt panic start to pull at her stomach, and she felt her heart start to ache. Her eyes darted around the room, trying to find something, anything. Off in the right corner she noticed a rusted old bed, and it wasn't until she focused her eyes to accommodate for the darkness surrounding the bed that she noticed a figure sitting on it.

"Oh, thank God. You have to help me." Elandra struggled against the ropes. "You have to untie me."

The figure sat there in a stone silence, sending Elandra into a deeper panic. She strained against her prison and felt her heart constrict even further. Elandra felt her breath hitch and herself start to hyperventilate.

"Oh, my, God," she wheezed.

The figure from the bed bolted up and raced across the room to her. "Come on, Cassidy, you have to even your breathing."

Elandra's head shot up as she looked at the man who approached her. "No! God no!" Her breathing hastened even further.

He crouched down in front of her. "Cassidy, you have to slow your breathing down, or you'll pass out."

Though Elandra's mind raced, she heard the concern in his voice, and her heart started an ache of a different kind.

He placed a hand on her right cheek. "Come on, Cass. You have to ease your breathing."

Elandra felt herself slow down her breathing to a more relaxed state, and she felt her shoulders fall as her tension seemed to fall away and her body seemed to give up.

"Where am I? What am I doing here? What happened?" Elandra asked, slightly frightened of the answers.

"I brought you back to me. Just like old times." He smiled, stood up, wandered over to the kitchen, and grabbed a basic mirror standing on the counter. He brought it over and held it up before her. "See, I even put us back to how we were."

Elandra stared into the mirror and took in her appearance—she looked just as she had when she was nineteen. Her hair was cut short, dyed blue, and placed in pigtails, just the way she had had it back then. It was back when she was in her rebellious phase, trying to find herself; when she was experimenting with her looks and how she felt about herself. She gazed down at the green tank top, which showed off her scar, and the low-rise jeans, which she couldn't remember having changed into. She glanced back into the mirror and spied the same type of snake arm bracelet she had worn all those years ago on her upper left arm. She stared back at her whole reflection and gasped. She had been transported. She looked exactly the way she had all those years when she had been first attacked.

"That's right, my little firecracker, just like old times. I brought you back to the Cassidy I knew. I found you again, and I got rid of all that pretend that was surrounding you. Now you're really my Cassidy again." He smiled up at her.

"But…no…it can't be you…" Elandra felt her heart rate start to quicken again, "They said…it couldn't be…"

"But it is. I told you I would find you again, and I did. I told you that you belong to me. Nothing will keep us apart."

"But they said…" Elandra shook her mind clear of her racing thoughts. "You were at a function. It can't be you."

"Function?" he asked, confused.

"They told me it couldn't be you. The chief said you were at the Children's Hospital Benefit." Elandra searched her mind for the answers.

"Hospital Benefit?" he pondered for a minute. "Ah, yes, that's right. Victor went to the Children's Benefit the night I found you again."

Elandra's head shot up, and she glared into his eyes. "Who the hell is Victor?"

"Why my twin brother, of course. The well-respected Senator Victor Prescott," he replied, putting on an air of sophistication.

"Senator Prescott?" Elandra squeaked.

"That's right, my dear: The man who admitted to being with the tramp, Chloe."

Elandra felt her blood being to boil. "Chloe was not a tramp."

"Well, what else would you call a girl who was paid for sex?" He gave a little laugh.

"She…she was misguided, that's all." Elandra said defensively. "Besides, how would you know what she was like?"

"Well, haven't you guessed?" He stood and pulled another chair in front of her and sat facing her. "He wasn't alone with her that night. Someone else was there, too."

"You? But why would you be there, too?"

"Well, someone had to silence her." He grinned menacingly at her.

"You…you killed Chloe?" Elandra felt her heart drop at the realization. "But why?"

"Someone had to stop her."

"Stop her from what? She was no danger to you."

"Of course she was. She worked for that bitch, Mercedes," he spat. "Mercedes had it all figured out. She took over when that idiot, Becky, was killed. There was no threat to them—no politician would out them. But they weren't just prostitutes, oh no. They were much too clever for that." Elandra watched as his eyes darkened with anger. "They worked only with politicians, and when those lazy, self-absorbed bureaucrats came for their fill, they would 'pump them for information,' so to speak." He paused to let her absorb what he was saying. "And that idiot brother of mine, Victor, let slip some tidbits that could ruin him. We couldn't let Mercedes get away with it, but we knew too many questions would be asked if we simply did away with her. So Victor came up with the brilliant idea to destroy her, so that her whole operation would be destroyed. We framed her for that girl Chloe's murder; that way, even if she denied it, which she was bound to, and told our secrets, who would believe a prostitute, let alone the madame?"

"But why kill Chloe? So what if Mercedes told his secrets? It's not uncommon for politicians to see prostitutes; it's accepted as common knowledge. Why destroy her?"

"Well, you see, Victor informed Mercedes about me. She knew I existed; it could have ruined us!"

"So what if people knew about you?" Elandra asked, wanting to know more.

"Think about it, my little firecracker. If everyone knew about me, then I couldn't have anymore playmates."

"You mean you couldn't rape anymore women," she growled.

"Oh, Cassidy, we always just played. You can't imagine the rush I got from having all those women squirm under me. Feel them fight me, and their screams— oh you could never imagine what those screams do to me." His breathing quickened. "But you were always my favorite, Cassidy. There was never anyone like you." He stood and moved toward her chair.

Elandra pushed back against the chair, trying to squirm away, but the it wouldn't budge. Elandra gasped as he leaned in, placed his face by her ear, and sniffed deeply, trying to fill his senses with her smell.

"No one ever made me hard like you, Cassidy. You were my first, and you'll always be my favorite." He sat back in the chair. "And Victor can never take you away from me."

Elandra straightened her back, trying to find strength and courage. "Why would Victor take me away?"

"He doesn't understand, he can't understand. He has Leila, he doesn't understand." He cast his eyes to the side.

"Leila. That's right, she's the one who brought the senator to us."

"Yes. Leila introduced Victor to your stupid school. When they married, she took control of him and took him away from me." He brought his gaze up to meet Elandra's. "But I'll say this: She did end up leading me back to you."

"Does Leila know about you?" Elandra felt her chest grow tight with the tension rolling off him.

"How could she? I don't exist." He chuckled. "I'm the twin no one knows about, not even our mother."

"But, how could no one know about you?" Elandra asked, trying to buy time.

"Victor came to my rescue one day. A group of 'bullies' from my high school had ganged up on me." He drew a deep breath. "Victor just happened along, and he helped defend me—he had been drawn to me by our unspoken bond. After that, we became fast friends, and with time, Marie came to tell me the truth of my family."

"Who's Marie?" Elandra asked.

"She was the woman who raised me." He smiled.

"What do you mean the woman who raised you? She wasn't your mother?" Elandra asked.

"No, Marie wasn't my biological mother. She was the angel who stole me away from my mother."

"She stole you?" Elandra shook her head in disbelief. "She stole you from your own mother, and you think she's an angel?"

"My mother couldn't look after both me and Victor. She wasn't capable. So instead of letting me enter the foster system, Marie took me in. She knew it would break my mother's heart to know that she would have to give up a child, so Marie stole me without letting my mother know I even existed. Marie saved me from the system. She raised me like her own. And when the time came, she told me about my blood family, letting me decide for myself."

"So what happened when Marie told you that you had a twin brother?" She silently strained against the ropes.

"That new history made my bonds with my parents and Victor stronger. Victor helped to make me strong and build muscle. When I was eighteen, my family was in a car accident. My father was killed instantly, and I was forced to sit back and simply watch Marie die." He looked at the ground. "Before she died, though, I promised her that they would always be my parents and no one else. So we never told anyone about Victor and I being twins, and the world went on not knowing I exist."

"So you decided, just like that? That you didn't exist?" Elandra stilled her movements, lost in his story.

"I couldn't do that to Marie. I couldn't let her lose her son." He looked up at her, his eyes full of emotion. "There was so much that I was never going to be able to give her. She knew she was dying. She knew she would never get to see any possible grandchildren—watch me grow up. She knew she was never going to even see me graduate high school." He placed his hands on her knees. "The only thing I could give her was the promise that I would always be her son."

Elandra looked at him with tenderness. "But you would still be her son, even if people knew."

He shook his head solemnly. "No. Victor warned me what would happen if I ever told. He said what they did was extremely illegal, and even though they were dead, their names would be dragged through the courts." He looked at her with pleading eyes. "Don't you see? I could never do that—I could never do that to her. I was protecting her, like she had always done for me." He sighed and leaned back in his chair, cracking his knuckles. "Do you understand? I could never tell anyone...I just couldn't do that to Marie."

His eyes pleaded for Elandra's understanding, and while her heart reached out to him, her mind waged war.

He raped me! But he loved her so much. *He's kidnapped me and tied me to a chair!* But he's done everything out of respect for her. *He raped me and will probably try to again!* But he did everything because of his love for his family. *His family? What about mine? He chased me from my family.* But he gave his life up for his. *He will rape me again, and this time he may kill me!*

Elandra's heart and mind warred on. The room was so thick with emotion that neither heard the door open.

"You understand, don't you?" his eyes were watery with unshed tears.

Elandra nodded as a single tear rolled down her cheek. "You gave up your life out of loyalty and love for your family."

"Yes," a voice sneered from behind her. "Loyalty is a funny thing." Elandra twisted in her chair, trying to face the voice, "Apparently it doesn't translate to blood relatives."

Chapter 30

Elandra twisted hard in her chair, trying to face the room's new occupant, "Who? Who?"

The man across from her rose from his chair. "Good, now I can introduce you two properly, though apparently you've met."

"What the hell is she doing here?" the new occupant growled.

The man before Elandra ignored him, walking over and turning her chair around to face the new occupant. "Cassidy I'd like you to meet the reputable Senator Prescott." His voice took on an air of false sophistication. "Victor this is—"

The new occupant cut him off. "Jacob, what the hell is she doing here?" He was trying hard to maintain his cool.

"Oh, come now, Victor, there's no need to be rude. Cassidy is here as my guest." Jacob turned back to face Elandra.

"My name is Elandra now," she ground out between clenched teeth.

"Jacob..." the new man's voice threatened.

Jacob waved off Elandra's comment. "Technicalities. You're back to you. You're back to Cassidy, Elandra doesn't exist anymore."

"Jacob!" The new man's voice echoed through the room like thunder.

Jacob turned back and faced the new man. "Yes, Victor?"

"I asked you, what the hell she is doing here?" Victor found it getting harder and harder to contain his anger.

"And I told you she is my guest. She belongs to me, and we belong together."

Elandra snorted in disgust, "Not in this lifetime, Jacob."

Jacob turned to face Elandra once more. "Oh, darling, don't say that." He walked up and kneeled in front of her. "This is just coming from that stupid detective." He ran a hand down her cheek. "He's poisoned you against me. But don't you worry, I'll take care of that."

"Jacob!" Victor bellowed once more.

Jacob swiveled around on his heel, placing his hands on Elandra's legs. "Yes, Victor?"

"I heard about your little stunt," he spat. "We were home free! They took the girl out of the way. We had nothing to worry about, but no, you had to go and risk everything over this stupid bitch!" He pointed at Elandra.

"I just had to make him understand, that's all." Jacob rose up to face his brother and stand between him and Elandra.

"That's all? You set fire to the guy's goddamn apartment!" Victor threw his hands up in frustration.

"You set fire to a goddamn police officer's apartment, Jacob!"

"They can't prove anything." Jacob crossed his arms in defiance.

"You idiot! You took her! You goddamn set an apartment on fire and kidnapped some slut!" Victor started to pace the small apartment.

"I've told you before, Victor. Cassidy is not a slut."

"They're going to ask questions. They're going to find us. He goddamn saw you!" He stopped abruptly in his pacing. He walked up to Jacob and slapped him in the face. "We're now in goddamn danger, you idiot!" He walked over to Elandra. "And all because of this goddamn whore!" He jerked his thumb at Elandra as he turned back to Jacob.

"I am not a whore! And you're right that you're in trouble. You have no idea just how much trouble you're in," Elandra growled at Victor's back, causing Victor to quickly spin around.

Slap!

Victor slapped Elandra across the face. "Shut up, bitch!"

Jacob stormed up to him, grabbed his shoulder, and pulled him back. "You asshole! How dare you!" he shouted at Victor.

Victor tried to push Jacob back off him, but Jacob kept pushing forward. Jacob grabbed Victor by the lapels of his jacket and shoved him back into the table. They struggled for a few minutes, trying to outdo each other. They twisted and turned, ending with Jacob's back against the kitchen cabinets. Jacob reached behind him and picked up a meat tenderizer, and with one final burst of strength, he pushed

Victor back. Victor fell backward onto the table, terror filling his eyes as he looked up at his brother.

"Jacob! No…" he gasped as he reached his hands up trying to ward off his brother.

Jacob pushed Victor's hands out of the way and brought his arm down with such force that the room shook. Elandra's head shot to the side away from them, and she squeezed her eyes closed, trying to block out the events unfolding before her. Her stomach rolled, and she felt all compassion for Jacob drain from her. Elandra sat in fear as the room grew quiet, and she could only hear Jacob's labored breathing. He drew himself up, tossed the tenderizer down on the kitchen counter, and wandered over to Elandra. He knelt down and lifted her chin with his now blood-spattered hand.

"Shh, baby. It's all right now. He won't say anymore awful things about you." Jacob's voice was tender, in complete contrast to what he had just done.

Elandra's eyes flew open, and she stared at him in disgust. "He was your brother."

Jacob stroked her cheek. "Shh, now, it's all right. Everything will be better now."

Elandra jerked her head away from his touch, her stomach rolling as she looked over at the still body on the table. Elandra felt her eyes water and fear grip her soul. "You murdered your own brother," she said barely above a whisper.

"I did it for you." Jacob looked at her in confusion. "I did it for us." Elandra turned her head back to look at him. "Don't you understand? I had to do it. I did it for us."

"There is no us!" Elandra hissed. "There never was, and there never will be!"

Jacob shook his head in a daze, "No, don't say that, darling. Victor can't hurt us or keep us apart anymore. We can be together."

"I would rather die!" she spat.

Jacob stood up, shaking his head. "We belong together." He walked over to Victor's still body and stared down at it. "I can be alive. I can have everything I want." He looked back at the kitchen counter and picked up the tenderizer again. He raised his arm. "Now I get to play the loving husband." He brought his arm down hard on Victor's lifeless skull.

Elandra stared at Jacob in horror. "What are you doing?" she screamed.

"I get to be the one who is alive now." He continued to bring the tenderizer down on Victor's head. "Now he gets to hide." He stared through the blood spattering his face and around him. "He gets to disappear. I get to be the only one. I remove his identity, and I become the only one."

Elandra felt the tears start to stream down her face as she fought to try to tear her gaze away. Elandra watched as Jacob stood up straight, dropping the tenderizer to the floor and turning to face her. Her eyes took in the bloody mass of bone and flesh that sat where Victor's face had once been. Elandra's stomach rolled, and she turned to the side and threw up on the floor. She watched as the room started to spin, and she felt her body go limp as she passed from consciousness.

Jacob walked over to the kitchen sink and grabbed a cloth, wetting it thoroughly. He walked back to Elandra and wiped her mouth. He stroked her face and reached around her, undoing the ropes. He caught her as she fell forward and picked her up in his arms. He walked with her over to the bed in the corner and laid her down gently.

He leaned forward and kissed her forehead. "Now we can be together."

Chapter 31

Kerith slowly started to stir, twisting his neck and wincing in pain. He pulled himself into a sitting position and rubbed at the back of his head. Kerith slowly got his bearings, and the pain in his head was quickly forgotten, for he suddenly felt the searing power of the bullet in his leg.

"Jesus Christ!" he swore, leaning back against the cabinets and pressing his palm into his bleeding leg.

He reached into his pocket for a handkerchief, but his hand came in contact with a small box. He pulled it out and stared at it for a minute. His eyes flashed recognition and he searched the room from his seat.

"Dammit!" he cursed and tried to pull himself up. But the pain in his leg was too much for him, and he collapsed back down to the ground. "Shit!" he swore as he fell.

Just as his butt hit the floor, the front door burst open. "Kerith? Reilly?" a voice called from the front of the house.

"Back here," Kerith squeezed out through clenched teeth, "in the kitchen." All Kerith could do was listen to the pounding of feet approaching the kitchen. "Luc." Kerith breathed a sigh of relief as he spotted the new occupant.

"Jesus Christ, Kerith! What the hell happened?" Luc took in the scene before him. "We got the call from Elandra, but she said you had the guy at gunpoint." He walked over to Kerith and handed him a handkerchief from his pocket, "Here. Where's...where's Reilly?"

Kerith nodded over at Reilly's still body. "He's out, but alive." He took the kerchief and tied it around his leg, he winced as he pulled it tight, trying to stop the blood flow.

Luc wandered over to Reilly's body and crouched down, "Jesus! What happened? You both look like hell. And...and where's the guy? And for that matter, where's Elandra?" Luc started to tend as best he could to Reilly's injuries.

Kerith gingerly pulled himself up, testing his leg. "He knocked out Reilly. We came to check it out and bastard hit me so fast I couldn't react." He winced and shook his head in shame. "He was so goddamn fast, it was unbelievable. He was able to knock me out, and when I woke up, both he and Elandra were gone. It was the same guy, Luc, the same guy who set fire to my place. The same guy who was after Elandra, and now..." he sighed in pain. "Now he has her." He carefully turned himself around to face the counter.

"Look, there's nothing you can do about the past, what's done is done. Right now we gotta look after Reilly and you, then we can go looking for Elandra."

Kerith's fist flew forward as he punched at the wall. "Dammit!" He glared at the new hole. "I handed her over to him. I gave her right to him."

"Reid!" Luc bellowed in an attempt to get Kerith's attention. "Look, beating yourself up isn't going to get her back here. It's not going to get her someplace safe, now we'll go after her just as soon we take care of you and Reilly."

"But he may kill her. He's obsessed with her, yes, but…" Kerith turned back around to face Luc. "But this guy is completely nuts. You have no idea. I…I just couldn't live with myself if she got hurt." He sighed, feeling his whole body ache from the thought. "And we…we don't even know where to start looking."

"Well look, we gotta wait for backup to get here, but…" Luc seemed to struggle with his words, fighting over whether he should tell Kerith or not.

"But what?" Kerith looked at him hopefully, "Come on, but what?"

"Well, Reilly told me you were looking into the senator. First off I think you're completely off base with him, but…"

"What? What!"

"Well, I helped Reilly dig, and we did notice one thing. The senator…well the senator has an apartment."

"So? What the hell does that get us?" Kerith ran a hand through his hair. "I'm looking for a place this psycho would take Elandra, not a new place to live!"

"The point is, you guys said the senator met that prostitute in a motel, right?" Luc watched as Kerith nodded his head. "Well his apartment is here in the city.

Why the hell would he meet a hooker at a motel if he has an apartment?"

"Where is it?"

"Thirteen-fifty-five Lilybrook Way. It's one of those crap apartments, in the rundown stretch by the old shipping warehouses."

Kerith nodded, "Yeah, yeah I know the place. We made a drug bust there a couple years ago. It fits. Yeah, it makes sense." He pushed himself off the counter, finding a renewed strength. "Thanks, Luc." He hobbled toward the hall, "Make sure they look after Reilly."

Luc started to rise from the floor, but his eye caught sight of Reilly starting to stir. "Kerith! Kerith! Goddammit, Kerith! Don't do something stupid, wait for backup!" Luc yelled down the hall, but it fell on deaf ears as Kerith was already out the door.

*

Jacob stroked Elandra's cheek, feeling the warmth of her skin and the fire it sparked within him. He gazed down at her, admiring her natural beauty. He smiled at her. He brushed at the dirt hugging her cheeks, leaned forward, and kissed her forehead.

"Silly earth," he muttered, smiling. "God decided to place dirt on you—his desperate attempt to make you look more human than you really are. You're really an angel, my firecracker; an angel sent to me from heaven." He kissed her forehead once more and stroked her hair. Jacob suddenly heard the pounding of feet coming up the hallway stairs. "Time to wake up, my little firecracker, we have company coming."

He waved a small vial of citrus oil in front of her face, and Elandra's eyes fluttered open. She blinked her eyes, trying to remember everything. Once her vision came back into focus, she stared up in pure horror.

"No, no…" she cried, feeling tears start to prick at her eyes. "Please, no! It can't be real! Please…" she begged.

"Shh, my darling. You have to relax, my firecracker. We have company coming." He reached his hand out to stroke her cheek but she pulled back.

Elandra screamed in terror, "No! No! Get away from me! Get away!"

The door flew open, and the bang of it hitting the wall echoed through the tiny apartment. "Elandra?" Kerith screamed from the doorway as he spied Jacob leaning over her. "Get the hell away from her!"

Jacob casually turned from his seat on the bed. "Come now. It's polite to knock before you come bursting into a room." He grinned.

Kerith took a step into the room. "I said get the hell away from her."

"Oh, come, come. It's not pleasant to order your hosts around. Did your mother never teach you manners?" Jacob continued to taunt as he rose to stand between Kerith and Elandra.

"Kerith?" Elandra sat up and tried to see around Jacob.

Jacob's grin fell away at hearing Elandra's voice, and he glared at Kerith.

"See? She doesn't want you," Kerith continued to growl, his gaze colder than ice.

"Oh, Kerith…" Elandra's voice trembled as she rose from the bed.

Jacob turned to face Elandra. "You would rather him?" he seethed anger. "You would rather have him than me?" Hatred rolled off Jacob with every word.

Elandra tried to steady herself. She drew a deep breath and met his gaze. "I would take him over you any day." Elandra felt some confidence return to her just knowing Kerith was there. She swallowed back the threatening tears. "I could never want you. I would rather die than spend another minute with you, Jacob."

"Jacob? Who the hell is Jacob? I thought you were the senator," Kerith asked, puzzled.

Jacob glared at Elandra, not even turning to acknowledge Kerith. "My senator brother is otherwise indisposed."

Elandra looked over at the bloody mess still on the kitchen table.

"What the hell is that?" Kerith asked, following Elandra's gaze.

"That's..." She hiccupped back a sob. "That's the senator."

Kerith's eyes widened in disbelief.

"He killed him, Kerith. He murdered his own brother." Tears started to fill her eyes as the fear came flooding back to her.

"Oh, dear God." Kerith swallowed back the nausea that hit him. Kerith tore his gaze away from the mess of bone and flesh.

Elandra's gaze returned to Jacob, and what she saw would haunt her nights. She saw rejection, pain, anger—but most of all, she saw hatred. Elandra fought hard to swallow her fear, and she raised her head in defiance. "I want to go home, Kerith," she stated with a confidence she didn't feel, not even turning her gaze from Jacob's.

Jacob's eyes darkened further with rage. In the blink of an eye, he stepped forward and slapped Elandra across the face. "You filthy little bitch!" he spat. "I offered you everything. I offered you the world. And this…this is how you repay me?" Jacob started to yell, turning his head away. "I gave you everything! I…I…" He brought his eyes back up to meet hers. "I *killed* for you." He brought his hand up to strike her again, but stopped as he heard the familiar click of Kerith's gun.

"Step away from her." Kerith raised his arms, training the gun on Jacob's back. "I said, step away from her."

Jacob turned to face Kerith. "Oh come now, detective. You must have some sense of justice." Jacob held his hands in the air. "You wouldn't honestly shoot a defenseless man." He grinned. "If we're going to settle this, at least make this a fair fight. Surely you can grant me that much."

Kerith snorted at Jacob. "I am nothing, if not a man of honor. Not that you deserve any. But seeing as how you're not laying another hand on Elandra, even if I have to kill you, I guess I can grant you that one thing."

Kerith turned his back to them as he placed his gun on the table, when all of a sudden, Jacob rushed him from behind, sending them both crashing to the ground. Elandra stood back and could only watch as the fight unfolded. She watched and winced as Jacob fell on top of Kerith; she flinched as they struggled and rolled around on the floor; her heart silently cheered when Kerith rolled Jacob over onto his back and sat on top of him, allowing his fists to fly at Jacob in a fierce fury. Jacob fought hard to scramble away by scratching at the floor, trying to drag himself backward. Jacob flung his arms back and felt his hand hit cold steel. He grasped it with all his being and wildly swung his arms. Elandra gasped in horror as she realized what Jacob had found, she couldn't help but stare as Jacob wildly tried to strike Kerith with the newfound tenderizer. Elandra watched as Kerith tried to lean back out of striking distance.

"What the fuck?" Kerith blurted out, trying to get a safe distance away. "Fair fight, my ass! You son of a—"

Kerith was cut off as he felt the strength of Jacob's legs kicking him backward. Kerith flew back and crashed to the floor and felt the air knocked from him as Jacob jumped to his feet. Kerith pulled himself up onto his knees just as Jacob took a step toward him, bringing back his arm as he did.

Elandra watched as Jacob towered over Kerith, the tenderizer held high in the air. Her eyes flew around the room and landed on Kerith's discarded gun. Her hand shot out to the table, and she picked up the gun. Without realizing what she was doing, Elandra aimed and shot Jacob in the lower back. He yelled out as he fell two steps back, arching his back in blinding pain. His arms folded up to his chest, and the tenderizer fell from his hand. Kerith bolted up from his spot on the floor and lunged at Jacob, knocking him back. Jacob fell with a loud thud as he hit the table and collapsed to the floor with the leg of the table arched into his back. Elandra's hand fell limp as she looked over at Jacob. Kerith knelt next to him, checking his wound.

"It looks pretty bad, but he'll live. Unfortunately," Kerith grumbled, looking back at Elandra.

Jacob coughed. "Oh, come now, detective. You…you want to see…see justice done, don't you?" he sputtered. "Want to see a…a murderer…go to prison…"

Kerith watched as Elandra took a step toward them, the gun wavering in her limp hand. "He's right Elandra. It's finished." He rose from the floor. "He can't hurt you anymore."

Elandra stared down at Jacob. "I lost my life to him." She leveled the gun at him. "He goes to jail, what then? He waits for parole and then comes after me again? No, Kerith." She shook her head. "I'm sorry I can't let that happen. I won't be afraid of him anymore."

Jacob coughed as he tried to laugh. "Sorry, firecracker, but you can't kill someone who doesn't exist."

Kerith took a step toward her, stretching his hand out to touch Elandra's arm. "Actually…" He watched Elandra as her eyes rose to meet his. "You took care of that. By killing your brother, you made yourself the only known Prescott."

Elandra watched Kerith's eyes, hoping she was understanding his meaning. He nodded his head, and she felt a strong confidence flow through her veins. She swallowed back the lump of emotion in her throat as she clicked back the safety. Elandra felt the pain of all the years Jacob had taken from her come rising to the surface; she thought about the family she had lost, the lack of safety she had felt, the pain he had caused her—but most of all, she thought of the time she had wasted in fear.

"I won't be afraid anymore," she said, her voice barely a whisper above the bang of the gun.

Her eyes filled with tears as she watched Jacob slump to the floor. She felt as if the world had been lifted from her shoulders; all her pain, all her fear was finally over. She didn't have to run. She didn't have to hide anymore. She stared down at Jacob's lifeless body and felt all the emotions just melt away. She felt as if there was hope; something she hadn't felt since before he had raped her. Elandra felt as though it had all washed away, and she wanted nothing more than to just walk away.

"Let's get you home. It's done now," Kerith said as if reading her mind.

Elandra merely nodded her agreement, tossed the gun down on the floor, and turned toward the door. Without a second glance back, Elandra walked out the door and away from the torment of the years behind her. Kerith followed her out and let the door quietly click closed behind them.

Chapter 32

"Oh, oh, oh! Wait, wait, wait! This is for our leader and ever-cherished boss. Elandra, you helped us find our hidden talents, and you help the world find their hidden desires." Gen raised her glass in a toast.

Everyone in the room lifted their glasses in appreciation, and the air filled with the sound of them clinking.

"And now, we party!" A cheer went up throughout the room.

Someone turned the stereo up, blasting the school's cherished song, "I Know What Boys Like." A line of girls formed at the front of the room, and they all turned singing and dancing toward the joyous crowd. Kerith's eyes floated through the room, falling on Elandra. He walked up to Reilly and Gen, his eyes never leaving her.

"So you broke your arm trying to fight off three guys?" Gen asked in disbelief.

"Yeah, it was brutal." Reilly rubbed at the arm housed in a sling. "I'm going to have battle wounds, but I did it to help innocent people."

"Even if El wasn't my best friend and she hadn't told me it was just one guy…" She gave him a disapproving glare. "I still wouldn't believe you. Psych graduates tend to be pretty good at telling when people are lying." She turned and walked away, leaving Reilly staring open-mouthed.

Kerith shook his head and laughed, tearing his gaze from Elandra. He patted Reilly on the back. "Better luck next time, my friend. Better luck next time."

Reilly laughed. "You're right. Next time is going to be much better." His voice was full of unspoken promise.

The room filled with laughter and light, and it was due to this overwhelming sense of excitement that Kerith was able to silently slip out the front door.

Kerith slowly walked down the street, trying to tell himself that it was better this way. She was right—she'd been attacked, her house had been broken into, one of her employees had been murdered, another had been arrested for prostitution, she'd had to go to a safe house, she'd been kidnapped from that very safe house, she'd been involved in the murder of a prominent senator, and she'd been placed in the clutches of an obsessed stalker. Yup, she had to be right. While he might not have been the direct cause of all these events in her life, they had all happened since she'd met him. She was safer not being with him, and she deserved better than being a cop's wife. *She was right,* he thought. *She was right, but why the hell do I not want to spend another day without her.* Kerith's thoughts were interrupted by the sound of a door closing, followed by the sound of high heels running down steps to the sidewalk. Kerith turned to see a figure walking toward him.

It seemed like thunder could be heard with every step she took. He felt the ground quake beneath him as she grew even closer. His hands began to shake; he tried to brush his fear away by running his fingers through his hair. He didn't know what made him more nervous, the determination and anger she walked with or the tight, black, three-quarter-sleeve boat-neck shirt, hip-hugging charcoal mini, coy tie choker, and boots that went up to her knee. Though the street they stood on held little light, as she drew closer these sparsely divided lights gave way to the expression on her face. The soft waves of her caramel-brown hair bounced gently around her face, but could not hide the fierce look in her eyes. His gaze darted around, searching for an answer in the shadows before him. He could feel his chest heaving as his breath became rapid and short, like he had just run a mile. He ran his hand through his hair again, searching for a way to calm down. He glanced down at the ground meters before him, listening to her thundering steps.

Then one boot came into view, and his eyes followed up her body, resting at each accentuated focal point; her hips, her neckline, and face. His gaze stopped at her eyes, her half-closed gaze overflowing with rage and seduction. He closed his eyes, fighting the temptation to give in, but as he felt her draw nearer, he decided he would face his imminent doom like a man. He took a deep breath and prepared himself, only to realize that she wore a small, sinister, yet erotic, smile. He gulped and felt his breath hasten once more. Now she was bearing down on him, mere feet away, showing no signs of stopping. As she came inches from him, he raised his arms to keep her back, but it was no use. Before he could say a word she pushed him up against a lamp post. She placed her hands on his chest and pressed tight against him.

"Look, I'm sorry. I didn't mean to…" He was cut short by her lips being pressed against his.

He pulled back. "Wait. I just…"

She stopped him again with her mouth on his. This time, he took both her arms in his hands.

He pushed her away gently. "Will you let me say my piece?"

Elandra huffed. "Fine."

"I'm sorry about everything that happened to you since you met me. And I don't want you to feel obligated." Kerith directed his gaze to the ground.

"Why would I feel obligated?" Elandra asked, confused.

"Well, because I rescued you from that psycho, Jacob." His eyes came up to meet hers.

Elandra crossed her arms and smirked. "You rescued me? I seem to remember saving your ass at some point."

Kerith took a step toward her, placing his hands on her waist. "True." He smiled. "But I think the breaking in and facing down the bad guy puts me ahead on the rescue scale." He pulled her closer. "Though we could always go and play rescue…" his words drifted off as he remembered himself and shook his head trying to clear it. "No, wait. That's not the point." He stepped back from her.

Elandra looked at him suspiciously. "What is the point?"

"The point is…" He turned away from her and ran a hand through his hair. "I think you were right."

Elandra laughed. "Well that's no surprise. I'm usually right." Her smile fell away when Kerith turned back to face her. "Okay, what am I right about?"

"About us not being together. You're safer if you're not with me." He dug his hands into his pockets, trying to stop himself from reaching out to touch her. "I mean, you don't want to be with someone you don't feel safe with." He looked down at the ground and kicked at a stone.

Elandra felt her heart swell. Here was this man looking like a chastised six-year-old, and all he wanted to do was protect her. Elandra smiled and decided to have a little fun with him. "You've got some nerve, Reid."

Kerith's head jerked up in surprise. "Excuse me?"

"You've got some nerve deciding what I feel, and especially what I want." Elandra had to work hard not to smile.

"I…I'm sorry, I didn't mean to…I didn't intend to…" Kerith sputtered, still reeling in shock from Elandra's apparent anger.

Elandra took pity on him. She shook her head and laughed. "You're an idiot sometimes, Reid."

Kerith looked at Elandra, confused. "I…I…I'm lost." He shook his head.

"I said all that, the 'not being together' and 'safety' crap because I was trying to protect you."

"You did?"

"Yeah. I thought you were getting into trouble and being put in the path of danger because of me. I just said it was your fault 'cause I knew you wouldn't want to lose your tough-guy image." She smiled.

Kerith's face took on an expression of pure relief. "Well that's just…" He reached out and took Elandra in his arms. "That's just…you don't know how great…"

"I wanted to protect you because…because I love you." Elandra's voice grew more certain with every word.

Kerith stuttered, a smile covering his face. "You do? You really do?"

"Yes." She looked straight into his eyes. "Now will you just shut up and kiss me?" She couldn't hide the teasing annoyance in her voice.

"Well, all you had to do was ask." He smiled at her.

He hugged her to him, their bodies coming perfectly together, her curves melding with his own. He devoured her in a deep and intensely passionate kiss. Their embrace continued on for several minutes, pausing only to come up and for air.

"Who are you?" he asked as he gazed into her eyes.

"I can be any of my teachers you want me to be," she cooed seductively.

"But I don't want one of your characters," he stated. "I want you. I want Elandra. I want you, now and forever."

Elandra gulped. "Forever?" she squeaked.

Kerith dug into his pocket and pulled out a small velvet box. "Yeah." He bent down on one knee, opening the box to her. "Miss Elandra Rosedale, also known as Cassidy Montgomery…"

Elandra giggled.

"Would you do me the greatest honor of spending the rest of your life with me?"

Elandra felt her eyes start to water. "Yes," she giggled. "Of course. Of course, I'll marry you."

"So, does this mean you trust me?" Kerith asked, trying to hide his smile.

"Of course. I trust you with all my heart."

Kerith smiled and removed the simple ring, placing it on her finger. "Whew," he laughed. "I was worried for a moment that I'd have to beat back other students."

Elandra smiled. "Well you'll have to if you don't get up here and kiss me," she laughed.

"Oh, yes, ma'am." Kerith quickly saluted her, rising and enfolding her in his arms. "Now let's make sure I do this right."

He swallowed her in a tender kiss, letting their bodies explore each other before he pulled back.

Elandra looked down at the ring, "It's beautiful, Reid."

"It was my grandmother's." He smiled. "It was the only thing I was able to grab out of my apartment before the fire and firemen destroyed it."

"Oh, Reid." Elandra looked up at him, letting all the love she felt show in her eyes. "I know it's a while away, but…" She smiled at him. "For our honeymoon let's go to Ireland. We can look for your brother when we're there."

"You really want to do that?" Kerith looked down at her with hope.

"Yeah. I want to meet what family you have left."

"God, you just keep getting more wonderful." He swallowed a lump in his throat.

"But of course I have a few plans for you before we go anywhere…" She let her voice trail off.

He pulled her close to him. "Oh really?" he chuckled. "Such as?"

She draped her arms around his neck and leaned back to look up at him. "Well, it's a surprise. But I will tell you I'll need whip cream, chocolate sauce, a camera, and a blindfold." She tilted her head, trying to look thoughtful.

"Jesus Christ, I want you so bad right now." Kerith's eyes turned black with lust.

A spark of joy lit up in her eyes, and she leaned forward, pressing her hot mouth against his neck, giving it little nips. He moaned as he gave in, this time, with this woman, he did not mind not being in control. If only for just this once…

About the Author

Jessica currently lives in Kanata, Canada, with her family and rambunctious dogs, Abby and Cassidy. She is currently the manager of the Fun Factory, a teddy bear building store located inside Walmart. When not writing, she's continuing school towards a Professional Writing degree. This is her first novel.